OBSESSED COWBOY

WHISKEY RUN: COWBOYS LOVE CURVES

HOPE FORD

Obsessed Cowboy © 2021 by Hope Ford

Editor: Kasi Alexander

Cover Design: Cormar Covers

CARTER

"How's it going, Ranger?"

I walk into the Whiskey Run Co-op and nod at the man behind the counter. Ranger used to work out at the Yates Ranch with me, but when the co-op needed a new manager, our boss Austin Yates got him on here.

"It's good, brother. How's it going at the ranch?"

I slow down as I walk up to him. "It's going. Everything is running pretty smoothly... probably a little too smoothly, if you know what I mean. It scares me a little."

He laughs and nods. I'm sure he understands what I'm saying. Hardly ever do things run smoothly on a ranch. There's always a sick animal, broken tractor, or something going on.

Ranger leans and rests his hands on the counter. "How about your place? I saw they put the footers in a few weeks ago."

I put my hands deep in my front pockets. Ranger knows what having my own land and house means to me. Austin sold me a piece of his land, and it's enough to get my own ranch started and to build a house on. I had hoped to be married and have someone to share it with, but when my wife, well, now ex-wife left me two years ago, I gave up on that dream. "Yep, footers are up, frame is up. They're supposed to start on electric and wiring this week or next. It's coming along."

He comes around the register and slaps me on the shoulder. "That's awesome, man. I'm proud of you."

I swallow, hard. He may not realize what his words mean to me, but they hit me hard. I was in the rodeo circuit from the time I was old enough to ride, only settling down when I had a leg injury and was told I needed to stay out of bull riding. I've worked at the Yates Ranch ever since, first for Austin's dad and now Austin. I'm ready to have something of my own. I clear my throat. "So, what about you? How's the family?"

"Good. Our youngest just turned two, and they're right when they call it the terrible twos."

He rolls his eyes and acts frustrated, but I know the truth. Ranger is definitely a family man and loves every minute of it. "That's good, man. Tell the missus I said hi."

He nods. "So what brings you in today? Did we forget something on your last shipment?"

We get regular deliveries out at the ranch ever since we switched from the co-op in Jasper to here. "No, I just need to get some rope and some finishing nails."

"Aisle three and aisle six. Let me know if you need any help."

I nod and stride across the store. When I get to aisle three, I turn down and then stop in my tracks. At the other end of the aisle is a woman with long chestnut hair. She's reaching up on the top shelf, her whole body extended. Her shirt has come up, showing the soft, curvy skin of her abdomen. I suck in a gasp and walk up behind her. I don't want to startle her, so I wait until I'm close enough to catch her if she gets off balance. Her jeans hug her ass, and I force my eyes off her ass to the back of her head. "Can I help you with something?"

She pauses before lowering herself to her flat feet and tugging her shirt down at the same time. "Yes, I can't reach..."

She turns as she's talking to me and stops suddenly. She lifts her head to look up at my face and snaps her mouth closed. I'm smiling down at her because how can I not? She's breathtaking. My eyes search hers just as hers do mine. There's not a word whispered between us, but I feel like the look she's giving me says so much. Her eyes are round and filled with innocence. The smile literally is lighting up my fuckin' world right now. When she doesn't continue, I take a step toward her. "Do you need help getting something down?"

Her hand goes to her chest, right over her heart. She's nodding and steps aside, averting her eyes back to the shelf. "Yes, uh please, I couldn't reach the hanging nails."

I move in, just because I want to be close to her. I take note of how her body reacts. She gasps softly, her breathing picks up into little pants, and her nipples tighten against her T-shirt. "Hanging nails?" I ask her.

She blushes. "Yeah, uh, I have a few frames I need to hang at the church."

I point at the nails I think will do the job. "These? Or do you need something bigger?"

Her blush deepens. Damn, she's pretty. "Yeah, those will work."

I pull the package off the hook and hold them firmly in my hand. I don't want to hand them over. Not until I know more about her. "Do you work at the church?"

She bites her lip. "Uh, yeah, well sort of. My father is Pastor Blake. And I play the piano." She blows out a breath. "And I just came home from college, so I haven't started a job yet."

I'm taking her all in, every blink of her eye and hesitant breath she takes. We have a connection, but I don't know if she realizes what's happening between us. She's young;

just graduated college, so she's probably twenty-two or twenty-three. I'm twelve to thirteen years older than her. I should hand over the nails and walk out of here... but I can't.

She tucks a loose piece of hair behind her ear and looks away embarrassed. "Uh, I'm sorry, I ramble when I get nervous. You didn't ask for my life story."

I almost reach for her and pull her against me. I want to... I want it more than my next breath, but I don't. She's skittish around me, like a just born baby foal. I put one hand in my pocket while the other one clenches on to the package of nails. "Honey, I want to know everything there is to know about you." Her eyes widen at the husky tone of my voice. I don't say it out loud, I wouldn't dare right here in the middle of the co-op, but I want to know everything—and I mean everything about her. The sound she makes when she comes, the feel of her bare skin against mine, her tight nipples against the hair of my chest, and the way her body expands around my hard cock. Fuck! I'm starting to sweat, and I rub a hand across my brow. This isn't good.

I'm about to be caught rock hard, right in the middle of the store with the preacher's daughter.

I shouldn't push, but I have to ask. "Do you have a man?"

She blinks and squeaks out a laugh. "A man? Like a husband?"

I reach for her then, grabbing her hand and lifting it up for inspection. I run my thumb across the bare knuckle of her forefinger. No ring. Thank goodness, because I don't know what I'd have done if she was married. I move closer to her, and I know it's too much when her eyes start to panic. I gently let her hand down and step back again.

She stutters the words. "No, I'm not married."

But that's not what I asked. Not specifically. "Boyfriend?"

She shakes her head.

I start to breathe normally after that. "Okay. What's your name?"

She laughs and tilts her head to the side. She grabs on to her long ponytail, pulling it over her shoulder as she runs her fingers through the strands. "Do I know you?"

"Carter Grant. I work out at the Yates Ranch."

I put my hand out, hoping that she'll let me touch her again. She does, but hesitantly. "I'm Janie Bradshaw."

"Janie." I breathe her name out.

She goes to pull back, and I squeeze it before letting it go. "Well, thank you for getting the nails down for me. I appreciate it."

Anything you want, I'm going to give it to you. That's what goes through my head, but I don't say it. "Yeah, sure, it's no problem."

She nods and almost gets to the end of the aisle before I stop her. "Oh, and Janie."

She turns quickly as if she's been waiting for me to say something. I keep my feet firmly planted where I'm at. I've already gone out of my way to touch her. There will be plenty of time for that in the future. "I'll be seeing you."

Her face lights up, and my heart starts to thump erratically in my chest. I've never responded to another woman like I am now. She nods and walks off.

I bend over, hands on my knees as if I've been sucker punched. In a way, I guess I have been. I never would have imagined walking in here and meeting someone like Janie. There's so much I don't know about her, but we live in Whiskey Run. It will be easy to find out.

I grab the items I need, but by the time I make it to the front, she's already gone. "Did you find everything?" Ranger asks.

I nod, looking out the front windows, hoping for another glance.

"Don't do it," Ranger says.

I turn. "Don't do what?"

He laughs as he bags my items and I sign the slip to add it to the Yates Ranch tab. "Don't even try it. She's Pastor Blake's daughter... young daughter."

I snarl my nose up at him. "What's that got to do with anything?"

He hands me the bag. "All I'm saying is she's not the play-around type. Don't mess with her. Miss Janie is a good girl."

I take the bag. "Yeah, got it, thanks," I tell him and stomp out the door. I about trample Drew, another friend of mine, on the way out the door. I nod my head at him but don't stop to talk. He won't mind, though; he's definitely not the chatty type. I can't get Ranger's warning out of my head. He acts like I'm old enough to be her father or something—which I'm not. And heck, it's not like I've been with anyone since the divorce or anything. I don't have time for that. And I know she's of age... she did say she's home from college. It doesn't matter. I'm not going to listen to him. I'm already planning on how I can see her again.

2

JANIE

I'M ALMOST RUNNING AS I LEAVE THE CO-OP. When I realize how ridiculous I probably look, I stop, huffing and puffing, and slow my pace down to a brisk walk. Did that really just happen? I ask myself. How had I never heard of Carter Grant before? How have I never met him?

I'm squeezing the bag holding the nails in my hand, and I swing it back and forth the whole way down Main Street toward the church. I pass Red's Diner and keep checking over my shoulder, waiting on the big, muscled man with the dark look-into-my-soul eyes to be behind me, but I don't see him. It's probably just as well. He's definitely more man than I would know what to do with. He's older, obviously more experienced. Dang, just the way he talks caused tremors in my body.

I keep walking, nodding my head when I see people I know. I don't know what to think, and I have a disagreement with myself the whole way to the church. He wasn't flirting with me... and then just remembering how he grabbed my hand and ran his rough finger over mine, well, my heart is still thumping wildly in my chest. He asked if I had a man as if he was ready to possess me right then and there.

I run up the steps of the church and through the front doors. I don't realize anyone is in the chapel until I hear my father's booming voice as he laughs. "No running in the church."

I stop and try to catch my breath as I turn, pasting a smile on my face. "I think I've heard that around a thousand times."

My father watches me and walks over to me. "What's wrong, Janie? Why are you flushed? Are you coming down with something?"

I can feel heat rush up my chest all the way to my head. *He doesn't know what you're thinking, Janie.* I try to look at him, but my eyes wander. My dad has always been able to know when I was up to something. Usually it's not been a big deal; probably the worst was when I was sixteen and Bobby Gilliams kissed me behind the church. I felt so guilty, I ended up confessing it all to my father. But this... gosh, there's no way I can tell him about this. Carter didn't even kiss me, but the way he made me feel just standing next to him, no I'm not going to talk to my dad about that. "No, Dad. It's hot outside, and I walked all the way from the co-op. I had to get nails." I hold up the bag for him to see.

He eyes me peculiarly. He knows something is up. Mostly because he's good at his job. He can read people and always wants to offer his help. But I can't ask him for help on this.

"Do you need help hanging the pictures?"

"Uh, sure, that'd be great!"

He follows behind me and into the back where the dining hall and offices are. I pick up the hammer and hand it to him. He laughs good naturedly. "So that's how it is. I offer to help, and I do all the work."

I put my hand on my hip. "Don't even play, Dad. I know as soon as I lift up the hammer or try to hang the picture you're going to take over anyway. You know I can hang a picture, right?"

He goes about opening the nails and hammering one in while I show him where I want it. "I know you can. I taught you how. But while I'm around, there's no reason for you to do it."

I take the hammer as he picks up the heavy frame and hooks it on the wall. I'm fortunate in a lot of ways, I know I am. My father is great and has always been here for me. When my mom passed away when I was fifteen, my whole world changed. I was devastated. My father made it bearable, though.

He stands back and looks at the picture before straightening it a little. When he seems to think it's okay, he turns to me. "Okay, so what do you think? Good?"

I nod. "It's perfect."

"Okay, two more."

He works on the next two, and since my job is pretty mindless, just handing him nails and the hammer, I seem to get lost in thought. I couldn't stop thinking of Carter even if I tried. There are so many things I want to know about him. I wonder if my dad knows him, I wonder how old he is and where he works. I'm guessing he's a rancher. All of it would be easy to find out; I could literally ask anyone in Whiskey Run, but as soon as I do, it will be all over town that the innocent preacher's daughter is interested in him, and let's face it, he's way out of my league. I sigh, somehow wishing I was different.

"Okay, what is it?"

My eyes snap to my father's. "What's what?"

He points to the wall where he's finished hanging all the pictures. "Well, I'm done. All the pictures are hung, and for the last two, you've ignored me when I've asked you if they're straight, so obviously there's something on your mind. What is it?"

He's smiling at me the way he always does.

He's patient, packing the nails up and putting the hammer back in the toolbox. I could lie to him, but I don't want to, and he'd probably realize it.

"How did you know? I mean, when you met Mom, how did you know she was the one?"

He starts to laugh softly. "Well, that didn't go where I thought it was going." He starts to walk, and I follow behind him. I know my father well enough to know that he's thinking about it before he answers me. He's always cool and calm, so as soon as we get into his office, I sit in the seat across from his desk.

"Well, let's see," he says, sitting down across from me. "I met your mother at a drive-in, and not like the movie drive-in, but the food place, where you pull in and they come to your car to take your order. Man, I miss that place. They made the best peanut butter shakes on the East Coast."

"Better than at Red's Diner?"

He shakes his head. "Don't you dare tell Violet I said that. She gives me a slice of pie every time I go in there, and I definitely don't want to get on her bad side."

I turn sideways in the seat and lay my head back. "I promise."

"Well, your mom was the carhop. She came out and asked me for my order. I asked for her phone number instead."

"Did she give it to you?" I ask, even though I already know the answer. I've heard this story before many times, but it never gets old.

He shakes his head as he's staring at the picture of my mom on his desk. "No, not at first. She took some convincing. She was also dating someone else, so I couldn't really blame her."

"What did you do?"

His lips lift up in the corner. "Well, I went there every day to see her. Sat in my car and ate my peanut butter milkshake. I was relentless. I wasn't going to give up. She talked to me, and the more I got to know her, well, one day she told me she broke up with her boyfriend. I asked her to marry me that same night." He starts to laugh, and I swear by the look on his face, he's reliving that night right now. "She thought I was crazy, but she did accept my request for a date. We went out for two weeks before I finally convinced her to marry me."

I sit up. "So you knew when she broke up with her boyfriend."

He shakes his head, and his eyes meet mine. "Nope. I knew from the second I laid eyes on her that I wanted to marry her."

I blush when my father looks at me curiously. "So what's all this about?"

There's no sense lying to him. "I met someone today, and I don't know; it was different." I hold my hands up. "And I'm not saying he's the one or anything, I just, I don't know. He made me feel things I haven't felt before. Made me start thinking about you and Mom."

He picks up his pencil and taps it on the open notepad on his desk. "Who is this gentleman? Anyone I know?"

I roll my eyes. I have no doubt my father knows him. He knows everyone in Whiskey Run. "He's no one, Dad," I huff and instantly feel guilty. I shouldn't say no one, but I don't want to tell him who it is yet. This is something I want to keep to myself for a while. Plus, I may never even see him again.

"No one, huh? Well, this no one sure has you tied up in knots." He points at my hands, which are holding on to the sides of the chair. I look down, and my knuckles are white from holding them so tight.

I loosen my hold and roll my shoulders. "It's fine, Dad. There's nothing really to tell. I just met him today." And before he can ask me anything else, I'm jumping out of my seat. "Well, I have things to work on. Thanks for hanging the pictures, Dad."

"You're welcome, honey. And hey, Janie."

I stop in the doorway, paste a smile on my face, and turn around. "Yeah, Dad?"

"He'll call you."

"How did you—? I mean, I don't..."

He picks up a folder on his desk and walks over to the file cabinet. I'm glad he's not looking at me, because I don't want him to see the hopeful look on my face. "I know he'll call you. How could he not?"

I shake my head. My dad always says the right thing. I walk over to him and give him a kiss on the cheek. "I love you, Dad."

He pats me on the shoulder and pulls me in for a hug. "I love you too, honey."

I walk away, and I can't help wondering if my dad would still want him to call me if he knew who he is, especially considering the fact he's older than me. Oh well, I'll cross that bridge when I get to it.

3
CARTER

I SHOULD HAVE CALLED HER. I COULD HAVE easily had gotten her phone number from someone in town. It seems anyone I talk to tells me they know her and then instantly warns me to stay away from her. She's like the town's sweetheart, it seems. I only saw her for a few minutes and yeah, she looks innocent, but these days, there's really no such thing. And yes, I may be older than her and yeah, I should probably forget about her, but no matter how hard I try, I can't.

So after a week of trying to make myself forget about her, of trying to convince myself that I'm no good for her, I find myself here in town bright and early on Sunday morning. I run my sweaty palms down the front of my dark denim jeans. I have on my black button-down shirt and my best hat.

Even knowing my boots are clean, I still wipe them on the mat as I walk into the church. Pastor Bradshaw is standing in the doorway, shaking hands and saying hello as people walk in. I'm the last one in line, and the pastor doesn't even try to hide his surprise when he sees me. "Carter, well I wouldn't believe it if I didn't see it myself. You came."

I take my hat off and hold it in one hand as I nod and wrap my other hand around his in a firm handshake. "Yeah, well, you've invited me enough. I thought I'd come and check it out."

He nods, smiling from ear to ear. "Well, you're always welcome here. I've been meaning to come out and see you. I wanted to personally thank you for donating your time last month out at the Jamison's ranch. When Mr. Jamison passed, the missus didn't know how she was going to make it. She said you got everything running smoothly for her in less than a week. She said you trained the cowboys, set her up on automatic orders at the co-op.... well, son, you really helped her out. You're a good man, Carter Grant, and this community is lucky to have you in it."

I can feel the heat creeping up my cheeks. The way he's going on and on about me, I almost feel guilty. If he knew the real reason that I'm here in his church, he probably wouldn't be as welcoming. "Thank you, sir."

He releases my hand and claps his hands together excitedly. "Well, I better get up front and get things started. I'll talk to you after?" He phrases it like a question, so I nod my head at him. It's not hard to agree to it; I've already decided that I'm not leaving here until I get to talk to Janie again. A part of me is curious if my initial reaction is still going to hold true today. I mean, maybe it was just a weak moment or something. If it was just a blip in time, I may not feel anything when I see her today.

I go toward the front of the church and sit in the fourth row. I remember her saying that she played the piano, so I sit on the left side where I have a direct sight of the grand piano. Pastor Bradshaw starts and does a welcome speech. I sit here with my hat in my lap and try not to fidget. I don't know why I'm so on edge. It's not like I haven't been to church before. Anytime they've had cowboy church out at the ranch or at the rodeos I'm at on Sundays, I always attend. Of course, those are definitely more laid-back than this. But it doesn't bother me that I'm in my new tight denim, or the shirt that's buttoned up to my neck. No, I'm anxious because I'm about to see Janie. There's someone else at the piano and the song service continues as people take their seats.

Pastor Bradshaw starts talking, welcoming everyone. I tell myself to pay attention, but I find myself looking around the congregation, hoping for just a glance of Janie.

His sermon continues as he talks about forgiving old hurts and not holding grudges and following your heart. I listen, but the whole time, I'm searching for her.

"And now, well, I'm sure you already know that my Janie is back from college. She took a few college classes this summer and was able to graduate early." He turns to the side and looks at a column along the wall. "Janie, will you please come say hello and play for us."

She has been sitting there the whole time. I watch, holding my breath for her to come into view, and when she does, I don't even try to hide the gasp that leaves my lips. She's breathtaking. She has her hair down today, and it's in curls down her back. She has on a white dress that comes to her knees with a purple short-sleeved shirt over it. She smiles shyly at everyone, and her whispered "hello" is barely audible. Nothing like the loud and robust "Hello, Janie" from the crowd.

She sits down at the piano and takes a deep breath. Her back is straight, and from where I'm sitting, I have a perfect side view of her. Her hands move softly across the keys, and the slow melody that fills the room has me sitting completely still, because I don't want to miss one second of it. When she opens her mouth and starts to sing, I grab on to the back of the pew in front of me. Her voice is the voice of an angel. She sings the lyrics, and the way she closes her eyes, I know that she feels the words to her very core.

I stretch my legs out in front of me and shift. I know I shouldn't. Damn, I know I shouldn't. But watching her, hearing her... it's just all too much. I adjust myself and don't even try to be discreet about it. My cock is hard in church. I'm sure it's a sin, and I'm probably going to go to hell for it, but there's absolutely nothing I can do about it right now. I can try to think about the last flood that took out twenty percent of the Yates calves, I could think about the hell of being raised in foster care, or I can try and think about the day I broke my leg and my rodeo days were over. All of those were horrible days, but nothing, absolutely nothing is going to let me take my mind off of Janie Bradshaw as she sits fifteen feet away, looking like that and singing like that.

When she stops, everyone claps. I know I should be. But I don't. I'm still clasping the pew in front of me with one hand, my other hand holding tightly to my groin, and when Janie looks out to the crowd with bright red cheeks, she looks straight at me. She gasps, and her eyes widen, but she doesn't look away. She looks straight at me, and I can feel the heat from her gaze as if she's standing right next to me.

As if in a trance, the room quiets around

me, but I don't dare take my eyes off her. I knew it would be like this. It wasn't a fluke, a crush, or a simple attraction. This is a gut punchin', heart thumping, got to have her temptation. I need to feel her under me and against me, and I need to be inside her as much as I need my next breath. I almost get up until Pastor Bradshaw walks over to her and pulls her up from the bench she's sitting on. "Now everyone, the monthly potluck is today, and since the weather is so nice, we have everything set up in the south lawn. And don't you worry, even if you weren't able to bring anything today, there's enough for everyone."

As soon as he finishes, Janie slides out from under his arm and walks swiftly toward the back rooms. I want to follow her, and I plan to do exactly that. I pick up my hat from the seat beside me and make my way toward the front. The pastor is busy talking to random people that came up to talk to him, so I am sure I can make it to Janie without him seeing me. I make it three steps before he calls to me. "Carter, can I see you for a minute?"

I stop dead in my tracks and watch as he

says something to a couple standing next to him and walks toward me, a smile on his face.

"I hope you'll stay for the potluck."

"Uh, well, I mean, I didn't bring anything," I stutter uncomfortably.

He puts his hand on my shoulder. "There's more than enough. The ladies have been working all week on this."

I nod but still don't commit. "Let me ask you something," he says.

My forehead creases, worried where this is going. "Uh, sure." *Please ask me to volunteer or something. Please don't ask me about your daughter*, I say to myself. I'm a grown man, thirty-five years old. I can handle dealing with a parent of someone I'm dating, but I don't know if I'm ready for this yet.

"By any chance did you meet my daughter? At the co-op, I mean?"

I purse my lips, knowing I need to tell the truth even though I don't really want to. "Uh, yeah, I did actually. Earlier this week." She must have told him about meeting me. I'm waiting for the warning to stay away from her or for him to tell me I'm not good enough. I put my hands in my front pockets, waiting for it.

He tilts his head to the side and looks up at me. "My daughter's important to me."

I nod. "I'm sure she is. She's... special," I tell him without even blinking. I barely know her, but I know it's the truth. She can't light up a room and sing like an angel and not be special.

He squeezes my shoulder. "Good. I'm glad you realize it. She's been a little down this week."

"Why? What happened?" I ask him fiercely. Did someone mess with her or upset her? Just the thought of it has me pissed off and ready to fight.

"Well, she wouldn't talk to me about it, but I told her that the guy she met... well, I'm sure he would call her.... He, well, you didn't call her."

I clear my throat. "And you would be all right with me calling her?"

He finally releases my shoulder and pats it. "I told you that you are a good man, Carter. Just don't prove me wrong."

I nod in understanding. "I won't, sir."

"Call me Blake. Now let's go and eat."

I look toward the back, and he sees me. He pushes me toward the front of the church. "Come on now. Janie will be out in a few minutes."

I don't have any choice to follow him out. I've waited almost five days to see her; surely I can last another few minutes.

4
JANIE

I KNEW THROUGH THE WHOLE SERVICE, listening to my father's sermon, that there was something different about today. I sat there the whole time trying not to let my mind wander, but no matter how hard I tried, I kept going back to the other day when I met Carter at the co-op.

He never called. I didn't expect him to; it's not like he asked me for my phone number or anything like that. But I really expected to see him. However, not at church. As soon as I sat down at the piano, I could feel his eyes boring into me, and I knew it was him. I felt the exact same when his eyes were on me at the co-op. I struggled with the notes at first, but finally found my footing at the piano and eventually was able to lose myself in the music. I barely ended the last note, and I turned my head to find him in the congregation. I didn't have to search long or hard. He was right there and so close I could feel the heat spreading through my body. After a quick nod for the applause and my father started the closing sermon, I was out of there.

I walked as fast as I could without drawing attention to myself. As soon as I got to the back door, I entered the secretary's office and shut the door behind me. She has a private bathroom, so I go in there and shut that door too. My palms are sweaty, my heart's racing, and there's a tug in my lower belly that doesn't feel like I'm sick, but I really can't explain it. I feel like I'm having a panic attack, but I know I'm not. I lift my eyes to the mirror over the sink and suck in a breath. My hair has come loose and is framing my face. My eyes are huge in my pale face, and I turn side to side, trying to figure out what's different about me but not able to really tell. I look at my dark brown eyes with the flecks of gold that stared back at me my whole life. That's what's different. They're darker. I move closer to the mirror, turning my face side to side, all the time staring at my eyes. They're hooded, and I gasp, covering my mouth with my hands. I'm turned on. That's what I'm seeing. The sweaty hands and the weird rhythm of my heart—it explains it all.

I put my hands on the sink's edge and lean on it, mesmerized by the look on my face. If I walk out to the potluck, are people going to notice it? Will they know what I'm thinking or what I'm feeling? Is it really that noticeable? Will Carter see it?

I shake my head. He's probably already gone.

I straighten my spine. I know I can't hide in the bathroom all day. I'm supposed to be helping host the meal. I straighten my cardigan, run a hand through my hair to smooth the edges, and paste a smile on my face. *All right, Janie, you can do this*.

I walk toward the door, open it, and almost immediately slam it again. I lean against the hard wood and lay my head back. I might need another minute... then I'll go out there.

Carter

As soon as Pastor Blake and I get outside, someone comes to talk to him, and I'm partially thankful for it. I know he's curious about my intentions toward his daughter, and right now, I don't know how I can explain it.

"Excuse me. Are you Carter Grant?"

I turn my head toward the voice and barely am able to hide my reaction to who's coming toward me. I've heard of Gina Johnson. I've even seen her in town plenty of times, but I'm usually able to avoid her. She's dressed all in pink with her low-cut blouse and short skirt. The strong odor of her perfume hits me before she gets within ten feet, and I look around, hoping that I can get away, but just as quickly as I turn, she has her hands gripping my arm and her nails digging into my skin. She's at least fifteen years older than me, and I've always been taught to respect your elders, but maybe I can get away and make her think I hadn't heard her or something. "Carter, you must not have heard me. I'm Gina Johnson and I'm part of the church's welcoming committee. Now I've saved you a seat right over here at my table." She starts pulling me with her, and I go, albeit reluctantly. I already feel like I stick out like a sore thumb; I don't want to draw any more attention to myself.

I walk beside her and sit down in the seat she all but pushes me into. I'm a big man, so the fact she is forcing me into the seat is definitely saying something. "Gina, thank you, really, but..."

"No buts about it. Now you sit here and I'm going to get you a plate." She pats my shoulder like I'm a child, but I've heard all about Gina. Her intentions toward me are anything but on the up and up.

She walks off before I get a chance to talk her out of it. I look around the table at the three women all sitting here with their smiles and fancy looking hats. They're eyeing me, and I nod my head at them before looking around at the rest of the picnic tables that are set up on the lawn. I'm trying to find Janie, but I feel it in my gut that she's not out here. I would know... I would feel it.

It isn't long before Gina is back and sets down a filled plate in front of me. Pulled BBQ chicken, baked beans, cole slaw, and a big glass of sweet tea. "Thank you, really, but I can't..."

"Nonsense now Carter. You go ahead and eat. You don't want to hurt our feelings, do you?"

I shake my head. "No, ma'am."

I pick up the fork and start to eat as everyone at the table stares at me. Any other time I would wolf this down without a second thought. My rumbling stomach tells me I should eat it, but I'm too off kilter and on edge, and I don't think it's going to get better until I talk to Janie.

I thank the ladies for their food and respectfully keep eating while I continue to search the yard for any sign of Janie. Ginger continues to talk and she's moved her seat as close to me as she can get. I act like I'm listening, that is until I feel the small hairs on the back of neck stand up and I know—I feel it to my very core—that Janie is here.

I look around again, and I spot her almost instantly. She's standing at the buffet table. She touches the shoulder of a woman, and they smile at each other as the other woman hands her the serving knife and Janie takes over the job of handing out pie. I sigh, thankful that I finally see her and that she didn't just leave before I could talk to her.

I watch as she puts a slice of pie on a man's plate. He stands in front of her a little too long for my liking. She's smiling at him and even giggles at something he says. I clench on to the fork in my hand and stare straight at her. As the man walks away, she looks at me. I try to relax my fierce gaze, but it's too late. She frowns at me, and her eyes look beside me and then back again before dropping to the table in front of her.

I stand up, done with all the niceties. "Ginger, thank you for the meal. I truly appreciate it, ladies, but I'm going to go get some pie."

"But you haven't finished eating."

I smile at her, trying to soften the blow. "I have sort of a sweet tooth."

She puts her hand on my shoulder. "Well, stay put, I'll get it for you."

"No! I mean, no, that's okay. I need to talk to Janie anyway."

I see the shocked looks on their faces, but I don't care. I thank them again and walk over to the buffet table. Nothing is going to get between Janie and me now. I'm going to talk to her if it's the last thing I do.

5

JANIE

I SHOULD HAVE JUST STAYED IN THE CHURCH. If I'd done that, I wouldn't have to see Ginger pawing all over Carter. And well, it doesn't seem like he's enjoying it all that much, but he has to know what Ginger's reputation is like. Of all the people here, why is he sitting with her? I try to hold in my disappointment. I take a deep breath and sigh.

"You sang and played beautifully, Miss."

I smile at the cowboy in front of me. He's blond, blue-eyed, and close to my age. If I'd seen him last week, I'd probably have been more interested in talking to him. But not now, not after meeting Carter earlier this week.

Darn, I can't let him ruin me for all men. We just talked. That was it.

I hold my hand out to the cowboy. "Thank you! I'm Janie."

He wipes his hand down the front of his shirt before grabbing mine in a firm handshake. "Hi. I'm Tommy."

I nod and pull my hand back quickly, trying to ease my reaction by smiling up at him. "Well, we're glad you came today. Here's a piece of pie. We hope to see you next week."

He takes the pie but doesn't move on. He's staring at me, and I know he's about to ask me out. I just know it.

I chance a look at Carter and he's staring right at me. I can feel the heat of his gaze all the way over here. I swallow and my gaze falls on the woman next to him. Of course, he's only been here one day and the single ladies of the church have already pounced on him. I sigh and pull my eyes off him and back to what I'm doing.

"Can I get a piece of pie?" an elderly man asks from behind Tommy.

"Yes, you absolutely can." I focus all my attention on him, and finally Tommy walks away. "Would you like apple or blackberry pie?"

"Apple."

I nod and put a big slice on the old man's plate. "Enjoy."

"I will. Thank you."

The man is already shoveling a forkful of the pie in his mouth before he gets away from the table.

"Can I get a slice of pie?" Carter asks as he walks up to me. He doesn't stop in front of the table. No, he circles around it until he's standing next to me. It's either the dropped octave of his voice or the closeness that has goosebumps rising on my arms in this hot Tennessee heat.

I don't dare look up at him. I stare at the table. "Sure, you can. Apple or blackberry?"

"Did you make either of them?" he asks as he moves even closer.

My breath hitches. "Uh, yeah, I made the blackberry. But it doesn't look like it's very popular."

"Blackberry," he says and even though he's just naming off a type of pie, he somehow makes it sound sexual.

I cut a slice, put it on the plate, and hand it to him. "I would have thought Ginger would have gotten you a slice."

Darn it, I said that out loud. I told myself I had no right to be jealous, but here I am spouting off at the mouth. I bend over, wiping the nonexistent crumbs off the table.

"Janie."

"Yeah?" I say as I straighten the plates and plasticware that doesn't need to be straightened.

"Look at me."

I pause, paste a smile on my face, and stand up. "I'm lookin' at you."

His hat is low on his forehead, and the shadow makes his eyes look even darker. "Does it bother you that I was sitting with Ginger?"

I shake my head, ready to deny it, but he puts his hand on my shoulder and squeezes. "Don't lie to me. There's a lot of things I can handle, but lying isn't one of them."

I jut my chin at him in defiance, but I know I won't lie to him. "Yes, it bothers me. But it shouldn't. I don't have the right—"

He interrupts me before I can finish. He

sets the pie down, and his hand goes up the curve of my neck, and he holds on to me there. "You may think you don't have the right, but I disagree. I didn't like seeing Tommy Cavanaugh talking to you either."

I blink as his thumb strokes across the pulse point on my neck. My heart is going wild in my chest. "Who's Tommy Cavanaugh?"

His lips lift in a smirk. "The cowboy you just served pie to. The one that wanted more than pie."

I can feel the heat rise on my face, and I look around at the people around us, wondering if anyone heard what Carter just said.

"Does that surprise you? You have to know you're beautiful."

I cross my arms over my chest. "I'm not, though. I'm too big. Men don't think of me like that." I'm not saying it to get attention or compliments; it's the truth. I've always been told that I'd be pretty if I lost some weight.

His voice is low and gruff. "If we weren't standing on the church lawn right now, I'd prove to you that I think you're beautiful."

My heart literally feels like it does a somersault in my chest. "I'm not, though."

I don't know why I'm insisting on arguing with him. Maybe it's because I don't know how to flirt back or what to say, so an argument is the way to go.

He moves even closer, and the smell of his cologne fills my nostrils. My nipples pucker against my bra, and I hold in a breath when he whispers, "You are. You're beautiful to me."

He wraps his hand around my ponytail and pulls a little, forcing me to look up at him. "Tell me you believe me, Janie."

I lick my lips. "What if I don't believe you?"

He inhales, pushing his chest out, and the hardness of his chest presses against mine. My nipples pucker painfully. I barely hold on to the whimper. "Then I'll be forced to show you that I'm attracted to you."

"How?" I shouldn't ask. I know I shouldn't, but I couldn't stop the question before it came out.

He tilts his head to the side. From this angle, if he pressed his lips to mine, it would be a perfect fit, but he doesn't do that. Instead, he lowers his voice. "Well, honey, if we were anywhere else, I'd bring your hands to me and let you feel how attracted I am to you."

I gasp. "Carter, you can't talk—"

He chuckles. "I know. So since I can't do that, how about we try this?" He drops his hand from my hair and grabs my hand, pulling it to his chest. My eyes widen in alarm. I shouldn't be touching him. I know I shouldn't be.

"Feel that?"

He has my palm right over his heart, and after a second I feel the thud of his heart. It's beating erratically, and I can see it jumping in his shirt as I look at his chest.

He pushes my hand more firmly against him. In a strangled voice, he asks again, "Do you feel that, honey?"

I nod, speechless. Carter Grant, the sexy older cowboy, is attracted to me. No, he thinks I'm beautiful.

"Can I get a piece of pie, please?"

I'm completely shocked and don't move fast enough. Carter squeezes my hand and cuts a slice of pie and hands it to the woman.

The woman blushes, and I can't help but feel irritated. "Is it always like that?"

He's cutting slices of pie and putting them on plates, arranging them around the table. "Is what always like that?"

I try to keep the frustration out of my voice. "Women... around you? They flirt, bat their eyes... I bet you date a lot, don't you?"

He shrugs his shoulders. "No, not a lot. I don't really have time to date. I just bought land and am having a house built, plus I work out on the Yates Ranch, so no, I don't really date."

Heat fills my body. *Don't say it, Janie. Don't say it.* "I guess these days you really don't have to date. I mean, you can get what you want without dating."

He lays the last piece of pie down and snaps his eyes to mine. "What do you mean? Are you asking me if I sleep around?"

I grab on to the sleeve of his shirt. "Shhhh! You can't talk like that... it's not appropriate."

He looks at me incredulously. "Janie, I'm pretty sure I'm just repeating what you're saying, but in a blunter way. I don't beat around the bush. But yeah, if that's what you want to know, I'll tell you. You're right; I don't always have to date a woman to get what I want."

"Ugh, right. Okay. Well, it was nice talking to you, cowboy. I'll see you around." I don't even try to hide my disgust. Since the pies are all laid out, I don't have to stay here any longer. Not that I want to anyway, not while Carter is putting images in my head of him with other women.

6

CARTER

WELL, SHIT. THAT DIDN'T COME OUT RIGHT. I
grab a slice of pie off the corner of the table
and trek after Janie. She's quick and on the
move, and I take time to appreciate the way
her ass shakes under her dress before I finally
catch up with her. "We're not done," I tell her
when I get in step beside her.

She laughs. "Oh, I'm done."

"Sit with me. Eat some pie, and we'll talk.
If you still want to go after that, fine. I won't
stop you," I tell her. I feel bad, telling her
earlier not to lie to me when I'm lying to her
now. I don't care if she wants away from me—
it's not going to happen.

She stops. "Fine. But if you start talking

about all the women you've been banging in Whiskey Run, then I'm outta here."

When she realizes what she said and how loud she said it, she glances around as if she's wondering if anyone heard her.

I wrap my hand around her arm, spot a huge oak tree with a swing hanging from it, and set her down on it. I cross my legs and sit down next to her on the ground. I have a perfect view of her legs, but I know ogling them right now is not going to help matters, so I concentrate on her face. I take a bite of the pie. "Wow, this is good."

She swings slowly, barely moving back and forth. "Thank you."

I take another bite and then another. It's really good.

"Do you want some?" I ask her.

She shakes her head, and I finish the rest of the pie in three bites. I set the empty plate next to me. "Okay, so let's get a few things straight."

She shrugs but doesn't say anything.

"Can you look at me when I talk to you?"

She rolls her eyes but at least does as I ask.

"Okay, so yeah, I haven't had time to date

and yes, I've been around before. But I don't know what that has to do with us. We just met."

She nods. "I know that. It doesn't have anything to do with me. You can do what you want. Are we done now?"

I put my hand on her knee. All right, obviously that wasn't the right thing to say. "Listen, I don't understand. It's not like I'm mad that you've..." I grit my teeth. "I'm not mad that you've slept with other men. It's not like I'm holding it against you or anything. You shouldn't hold my past against me."

Her mouth drops open, and she stops moving completely.

"What? It's the truth."

She shakes her head. "No, it's not the same thing. I don't sleep around."

I curse under my breath. "I'm not saying you sleep around."

She leans toward me. "No, I'm saying it's not the same because I'm a virgin." She pauses with her face red. "I don't have sex."

I start to laugh, but when I notice that she's not, I stop in shock. "A virgin? How old are you?"

She answers me through gritted teeth. "Twenty-two."

"Twenty-two... and you're telling me you've never had sex."

She looks around at the families, and I know the exact moment her gaze lands on her father. She straightens her back and pulls her knee from under my hand. "No, I haven't, and I don't want to talk about this anymore."

I drag my eyes off her. Her little revelation is affecting me in ways it shouldn't. How in the world can she be twenty-two years old and a virgin? Does that even happen in today's world? And why am I not running out of here? I should get up and walk away. I've never been with a virgin, but the way she's looking at me now, I know that she's not someone I can just have my fun with and go the other way. She's looking at me with forever in her eyes.

I wait for the sick feeling to come, the stomachache, the fear... something. But nothing happens, and I don't get up. As a matter of fact, I know there's no way I can walk away from her right now.

"Come with me riding?"

She holds on to the hem of her skirt, pulling it down over her legs. "At your ranch?"

I shake my head. "No, the Yates Ranch. Mine doesn't have any horses yet."

She crosses her arms over her chest, pushing her breasts up to the V-neck opening of her dress. I don't have a clue what is wrong with the men of Whiskey Run. How in the world is this woman still untouched?

"Did you hear me? I'm a..." She blows a breath out. "I don't sleep around."

I clench my hands into fists. "Good, I don't want you to."

"Well, that means that me and you... it's not going to happen. You'd have better luck with Ginger over there."

I don't even look over where she's gesturing. I'm sure Ginger's watching me, waiting for her chance to jump in. "I'm not asking you to go riding with me so I can have sex with you."

"Good, because it's not going to happen."

I grab on to the rope of the swing and pull her to me. "I want to spend time with you. That's all. I just want to get to know you."

Her nose is curled up, and there's

indecision clearly on her face. "C'mon, I promise. Nothing's going to happen that you don't want to happen."

She raises her eyebrows. "That doesn't sound too promising, Carter."

I shrug. "What, you don't think you can resist me?" I ask her while wiggling my eyebrows.

She tries not to laugh, but she can't hold back. Her giggle is soft and sweet sounding. "I can definitely resist you."

"Okay, so you have nothing to lose."

She's going to cave. I can tell by the way she's looking at me that she wants to. "Come on, Janie. Go riding with me."

"When?"

"Today."

She shakes her head. "I can't today. I have to help here, and then I have singles group and then church tonight."

"Singles group?"

She nods. "Yeah, it's a Bible study."

"For singles?" I unfold my legs, stand up, and move behind her. "Wrap your skirt around your legs, honey. I'm going to push you."

As soon as I know her skirt is secure, I start to push her. Just tiny nudges to get her going, but it gives me time to think. "I don't like it."

She looks at me over her shoulder. "You don't like what?"

"Well, usually a singles group is something where you go to try to meet someone."

She faces forward. "We're studying the Bible."

"Are there men there too?"

I'm watching the back of her head as she nods. Well shit.

"What time is the Bible study and where's it at?"

"It's a large group, so it will be here. At five."

I put my hands on her waist and stop her. "Okay, well I have to go and do some chores at the ranch if I'm going to make it back in time."

"Wait, you're coming? To the group?"

I take a few steps away from her. The way she's looking up at me with her wide, innocent eyes, I have to. Just looking at her makes me crazy. "Yes and to church after." I lean in and whisper, "If your daddy wasn't watching me right now, I'd kiss you, but it looks like I'm going to have to wait. See you in a while, darling."

I turn and walk away, waving bye to Pastor Blake as I go. I look like a man on a mission, and right now, I am. I need to go so I can get back. I have a feeling that I'm not the only one that's going to be vying for Janie's attention tonight.

7

JANIE

"I still can't believe you came," I tell
Carter later that night.

"I told you I was coming. Why can't you
believe it?"

We're sitting on my front porch, and my
dad's inside the house. I know he's probably
going to ask me what's going on with Carter as
soon as I walk in the door, so I'm happy to put
it off for a while longer.

"Uh, I also can't believe that you told
Tommy Cavanaugh to back off."

He turns in the porch swing so he's facing
me. "Really? He was acting like the two of
you were on a date or something."

I start to laugh because he's completely

wrong. "No he wasn't. He just asked to be my partner for the group."

"I don't share, Janie." His voice is hard and filled with warning.

Hope flares in my chest. He's making me want things I know I shouldn't. Things that I know I'm not going to get from Carter. He's a fun-time guy. I don't think he's the settling down type, and I already know, just in the short time I've known him, that he could hurt me. I can already feel myself getting attached. "There's nothing to share, Carter. It's not like we're a thing."

He threads his fingers through my hair. I showered after the potluck today, and I spent extra time curling my hair before Bible study tonight. I tried to pretend that it wasn't because I knew I'd be seeing Carter, but I was just lying to myself.

"When are you coming out to the ranch to go riding?"

I shrug. My schedule's pretty free. At least for now, until I get a job. I went to school and got a business degree, but I still am not sure what I want to do with my life. "I don't know. I need to apply for jobs tomorrow."

"What are you wanting to do?"

"You mean for work?"

He nods and rests his hand on my shoulder. It's hard to think when he's touching me. "You probably don't want to know."

He squeezes my shoulder. "Sure I do."

"I went to college because it was expected of me."

He widens his legs, and his thigh presses against mine. "So you have a degree in..."

"Marketing."

He nods. "Marketing. Okay, so what do you want to do? Tell me, I want to know."

I hesitate because I know how it's going to sound, but I also know that I might as well tell him. This way, he can hear it straight from me and we can both go on with our lives. "You're sure? You really want to know?"

He laughs. "Yes, I definitely have to know now. The suspense is killing me."

I pull my shoulders back and flex my fingers in my lap. "Well, I don't really care what kind of job I get. I'm fine working at the church or maybe the diner or the hardware store. I just want experience. I'd eventually like to do online marketing because I want to work from home."

"I don't get it. Why wouldn't I want to know that?"

I try not to fidget. "Well, to be honest, whatever job I get, I want it to be secondary. What I want is to meet a man. A good man that loves me and all the crazy little quirks I have. I want to get married and have kids." I hold up three fingers. "Probably three, two boys and a girl. I want to have family dinners and be a soccer mom. And well, every night I want to lie in my own house in my husband's arms and know that no matter what, I'll always have him by my side. That's why I want to be able to work from home."

His legs stop moving, halting the slow swing of the porch swing. The sun has gone down, and we turned off the porch light earlier when it kept attracting bugs. I can't see the look on his face, but I can imagine what it is. "I know, I know. I sound so outdated, but that's what I want. That's what I've always wanted. And I know it sounds like I don't want to work, but I don't mind working at all. I just —gosh, it sounds awful, but I want to spend time taking care of my family... that's what I really want."

He still doesn't say anything, and I wait for him to get up, make an excuse, and run out of here. My body jerks when I feel his hand on my lap, and he wraps his big hand around mine. "You'll get it. If that's what you want, it will happen."

"Yeah, so, uh what about you?" I ask him.

He threads our fingers together and pulls our hands over to his thigh. "You mean what do I want to do? Well, let's see. I want my own ranch and a house."

"You're getting those."

He wraps his other hand around ours until mine is being held in both of his. "Yeah, and I mean, I'm older than you. I'm not sure if I believe in forever and all that—at least it wasn't like that in my own family, and I was married before. When she left, well, I'm not sure I can trust again." He sighs and continues, "But I do want kids one day, so I'm not really sure."

I try not to let his words affect me. I start to think about him on his ranch, with little kids around him and working side by side with his wife. I shake my head to get the thoughts away. "You don't believe in being with someone forever?"

He grunts. "No, at least I've never seen it personally."

My thoughts go to my parents. They were so in love, anyone that was around them could feel the love they had for each other. When my mom died, it was so hard for my father, but he's content knowing they'll be together again one day.

I always get sad when I think about my mom, and I can feel the loneliness of it in my voice. "Well, I better go in," I tell him.

I start to get up, but he squeezes my hand to hold me in place. "Not until you tell me when you're coming riding."

"You still want me to go riding with you?"

"Yes. Absolutely."

"Carter, I think we both know this is not going anywhere."

He pushes my hair off my shoulder. "There's nothing wrong with getting to know each other."

I should tell him no, but there's a part of

me that really wants to go riding with him. "I can come Tuesday."

"When?" he asks immediately.

I shrug. "My schedule's pretty open until I find a job. What works best for you?"

"How about I pick you up around three?"

"What? No, that's crazy for you to come into town to get me and then have to bring me back. I can just meet you out at the ranch."

He stands up, pulling me with him. "I'll pick you up at three on Tuesday. Put your number in my phone."

He hands me his phone, and I put my phone number in. There's no reason for me to argue. He seems like a man that is used to getting his way. "Okay. I'll be ready."

I turn to walk away, but he stops me. His voice is hushed on the dark porch. "Janie?"

I stop walking but don't turn around. "Yeah?"

The sound of his boots is loud on the porch as he walks toward me. I can feel his heat at my back. "Look at me, honey."

I take a deep breath and turn at the same time his hands come up and wrap around the sides of my neck. I forget to breathe in this moment. "Can I kiss you?"

"Carter..." I start, knowing what my answer should be.

"Don't tell me no. Just a kiss. I just... It's going to sound ridiculous."

I turn my head to the side and look up at his face. It's dark, and the hat on his head gives even more shadows to his face. I have no idea what he's thinking right now. "What is it? Tell me."

"It's all I've thought about since I met you at the co-op. I want to know what it's like to kiss you."

I gasp and almost immediately feel inadequate. "I'm not a good kisser, Carter. It's not like I've had a lot of practice."

Even admitting that in the dark, where there's no way he can see my face, I can feel myself turning red. His hands tighten, locking together at the base of my neck. "That's good. I know it's not fair or right, but I don't like to think of you practicing with someone else. Let me teach you."

I wait half a second and nod. He doesn't waste any time as he moves his hands from my neck to cup my face. I freeze in anticipation, waiting for him to make the next move. I can feel his warm breath against my cheek and then his lips press to mine. I don't do anything. I don't dare move a muscle because the feel of his soft, firm lips against mine is way more than I could have imagined. He pulls away, and I whimper, not wanting it to be over.

He grunts to me, "Open your mouth, Janie."

He doesn't give me time to respond; he meshes his lips to mine again, and it's hotter, stronger and almost makes me delirious this time. I gasp, and he doesn't hesitate. He uses my shock to get closer to me, pressing his tongue into my mouth. My eyes pop open, but he doesn't stop. I may not know what to do, but I just let myself go and enjoy it. His mouth fits perfectly over mine, and the way he's holding me tight against his body, I can feel everywhere he's hard and I'm soft. Hard... his hips are against mine, and there's no denying the big bulge that is pressing into my belly. I pull away, panting and trying to catch my breath.

"Carter..." I start, not knowing what to say. Do I apologize or act like I didn't notice?

"Janie, I'm sorry. I've never had that reaction before... not that strong... not just from a kiss."

Just a kiss, he said. My goodness, if that was just a kiss, I couldn't imagine what would come next. "I'm sorry... I didn't know."

He grabs on to my hand. "Honey, you definitely don't need lessons."

My nipples are tight, my breasts heavy, and I swear I can feel warmth between my thighs.

His voice is almost urgent. "Go inside, honey. Go in."

"But... are you okay?"

He's a little bent over, and he's talking in a voice that is a pitch higher than normal. "I'm fine. Go in. I can't explain it now, but I will on Tuesday."

I start to walk past him but stop. I hate leaving him like this. "Are you sure you're okay?"

Frustrated, he sighs. "Janie, you have three seconds to put a door between us or I'm going to show you exactly how hot and bothered I am from little kiss you gave me."

A part of me wants to defy him and experience exactly what he's warning me about, but I know I shouldn't. I can't change all my ideals about sex after marriage after one kiss. "I'll see you Tuesday."

I all but skip past him and in the door. I'm breathless as I walk in, and my father is sitting in the living room with the television as the only light.

He peers at me over his glasses. "Janie, is everything okay?"

I do my best to sound calm. "Yeah, Dad. Everything's fine."

"Was that Carter Grant that brought you home from church?"

He knows it was. I told him before I left the church that Carter was going to bring me home. I wrap my hands together in front of me and wait for the speech. I know he has an opinion on how old Carter is, and I'm sure it's obvious how much more experienced he is then me. "Yes, Dad. We've been sitting on the porch talking."

He harumphs, and I know he knows that

we did more than talking. "Okay, Janie. All I'm saying is your mother and I raised you to know the difference between right and wrong. Carter's a good man... but I'm not sure he's the settling down type. Just be careful, okay?"

I nod, disappointed to have my own thoughts about what Carter said to me but also happy that it doesn't seem my father is going to try and forbid me from seeing him either. "Okay, Dad. I'm going job hunting tomorrow so I'm going to go up and work on my resume."

"Okay. Good night, Janie."

I tell him good night and all but run up the stairs to my bedroom. As soon as I close the door behind me, I lean against it. I don't know how I'm going to concentrate on anything tonight. The only thing I can think of is kissing Carter Grant and when I'll get to do it again.

8

CARTER

When I got home from dropping off Janie last night, I wanted to call her and hear her voice. I was still caught up with how I reacted to that kiss, and even though I wanted to talk to her, I felt like I needed to get my bearings. I've worked hard all day on the Yates Ranch, and by the time evening rolls around, I make my way over to my ranch to check on progress.

It will probably be another month before I'm even close to moving in, but I'm excited that my dream of having my home is tangible now. It's right here, and it won't be much longer.

I pull my phone out if my pocket and walk

to the edge of the property. From this location, I have a perfect view of the lake with the mountains behind it. I still can't believe that Austin sold me this piece of land, but I'm happy he did.

I open the contacts app on my phone and find Janie's number. I've almost called or texted her all day, and well, I don't want to put it off any longer.

I dial her number and bring the phone up to my ear. I pace along the dirt trail and kick a piece of gravel as I wait for her to answer.

"Hello?" she says, out of breath.

I can't stop the smile from forming on my face. "Hey, Janie."

"Carter. Hey, how are you?" she asks, and my smile gets even bigger when I hear the happiness in her voice.

"I'm exhausted. I didn't sleep well last night. I got bucked off a horse this morning. One of the tractors broke down, and one of the horses—a thoroughbred—is down with bloat."

"You got bucked off a horse? Are you okay? How's your leg?"

I grimace, realizing that she's asked about

me, and someone has told her about my injury that put me off the rodeo circuit. I hate the fact she knows. I don't know why it matters—I've never been sensitive to my injury before, but I hate for Janie to think less of me, like I'm not a capable man. "Yeah, I'm fine," I tell her, not wanting to admit that my limp is a little more pronounced today.

She pauses for a second and then asks me real soft like, "Do you want to cancel tomorrow?"

"Hell—I mean, heck no," I tell her, remembering that I need to clean up my potty mouth. I'm sure her being the preacher's daughter she's not used to hearing foul language all the time.

"If you're hurt, you shouldn't be riding a horse, Carter."

I pull back the phone and stare at it as if by doing so I can see what's on her mind. Is she trying to back out on me? I put the phone back to my ear. "You do know that I ride horses for a living. Right?"

She stammers, "Yeah, I mean, yes of course I do."

I grip the phone tighter. "Are you trying to back out on me?"

She's quiet and doesn't answer me. If it was anyone else, I'd let it go. I don't want to force anyone to be with me if they don't want to. "What's going on, Janie?"

"I just thought... well, I just thought that maybe now that you've had time to think about it, you've changed your mind."

"Changed my mind about what?" I ask.

"Me. I mean, bringing me out to the ranch. I know we're different, Carter, and I'm not going to be mad at you if you decide... well, if you think your time could be better spent."

I shake my head. "Where is this even coming from, Janie? I thought you wanted to spend time with me."

She's quick to respond. "I do. I really do, but I'm going to be honest because that's the only way I know how. I like you, Carter. My father warned me—"

I interrupt her. "I knew he wouldn't like us hanging out together."

She's quick to defend him. "No, he doesn't mind that. He just warned me that you may want different things than I do. He just doesn't want me hurt, that's all. And I've thought about it. I'm not experienced. I haven't really dated, and gosh, just that kiss made me feel things I'd never felt before." She pauses and then rambles on really quickly. "I'm just saying that being with you, spending time with you... I already know that you can hurt me, Carter, and I don't want to get hurt."

Everything she has said is right. I know it is. I want to settle down, I really do, but I just don't know if I can. I don't have the best track record with women, and I'm not going to commit before we've even been on a proper date. And what do I have to offer her anyway? I'm a broken-down cowboy. Yeah, I'm finally getting a ranch, but it will take years to get it to a point where I'm making decent money to where I won't have to worry. She deserves more than that. I shake my head. What am I even thinking? I'm acting like I'm about to marry this girl, and that's not going to happen.

"I don't want to hurt you," I tell her. There's so much I should explain to her, but I don't. I just tell her the truth. I really don't want to hurt her.

"Okay... well, thank you for telling me now..."She's trying to keep her voice flat and void of emotion, but I can hear the pain.

"Janie..."

"I'm fine... I understand..."

"Stop. You act like I'm breaking up with you or something. All I said was I don't want to hurt you. Look." I blow out a breath. Already this is way more than what I'm used to dealing with, but the thought of letting her go is like a sucker punch to the stomach. I can't. "I know we're different, and I know I'm fucked up, but I like spending time with you. Let me take you riding. We're friends... we can be friends, right?"

She hesitates, and I wonder if I offended her with saying fuck or if she's thinking I'm crazy right now, but eventually, she agrees. "Yes, Carter. Yes, if your leg is all right and you feel like it... I would love to go riding with you."

"Good. It's settled. I'll pick you up like we planned. And listen, Janie, no more trying to back out. I'm looking forward to seeing you."

Her voice softens, and my chest tightens at

the sound. "Okay, Carter. Me too. I'm looking forward to seeing you too."

Her words bring a whole new slew of images to my mind, and I try to tamp them down. I definitely shouldn't be thinking that, not with her and not right now. "All right, so tell me about job hunting today. Were you able to find something you think you'd like to do?"

She starts to talk about the applications she put in, and I listen to her talk. I walk across my land, soaking in the views and letting her voice wrap around me. There's a calm within me when I talk to her, but I don't want to think too much about it. I want her more than I've ever wanted a woman, but I know I can't have her. Not without the whole wedding and vows, but I can't let myself think that—not now, anyway. Plus, there's no denying the fact that she deserves more than I'm able to give her right now.

"... but so far, my most promising application was probably at Sugar Glaze. They are thinking about hiring someone to work part time in the evenings at the store and also to handle their social media marketing. The atmosphere was laid-back, and they were all so kind. Do you know they give a big discount to the police, fire department, and military? I thought that was so sweet when I found out."

There are so many things I hate about what she just said, but I can't say a word about it. I don't have that right. I put my free hand in my front pocket and roll front and back on my feet. So she would be working nights, and automatically I'm wondering when I'd get to see her, even though we just talked about being friends. And then she's telling me that they offer discounts and already I'm picturing all the policemen and fireman that would be coming in to see her, regardless of the discount. I drag my hand out of my pocket and rub my chest. I have a weird achy feeling and wonder if maybe it's heartburn or something.

Janie continues. "Of course, that's probably a bad idea because I definitely don't need to eat sweets. I'm already feeling sorry for the horse I'm going to be riding tomorrow." She says it jokingly, with a giggle at the end, but I still hate hearing it.

"Janie, you're perfect," I tell her point blank.

"I wasn't fishing for a compliment or anything. I know what I am," she says, her voice a little defensive.

"I don't want to hear you talk like that. I like you just the way you are, and I wouldn't want you to change for anything. You're beautiful inside and out, and even though I probably shouldn't say it, I'm going to..."

I pause because I know I shouldn't say. I know it.

"What? Shouldn't say what?"

"I shouldn't say that since I saw you at the co-op, you're all I've thought about. I know we're friends, and I'm not trying to change that, but I'm also not going to deny that I'm attracted to you. Your curves are..."

I stop, because I can't be crude with her.

"They're what... my curves are what?"

I sigh in frustration and run my hand through my hair. I'm thinking about the way her jeans hugged her ass in the store and the way her hips swayed under her dress and the way her breasts jiggle when she walks. "Your curves are beautiful. They make grown men ache like they're teenage boys again. I would plead and make deals with the devil himself to wrap my arms around you and hold on to your curvy hips, or to be able to pull you into my lap and feel your curvy body pressed against mine. So yeah, don't go complaining about the way you look, Janie because you're perfect just the way you are."

I said too much. As soon as I get done with my rant, I realize that I shouldn't have said it. But after not sleeping and everything today, I just said exactly what I was thinking. "I have to go," I say. I need to get off the phone before I do any more damage.

"Wait!" she says breathlessly. "So I'll see you tomorrow?"

"Yes. I'll see you tomorrow."

She's smiling again. I can hear it in her voice. "Okay, Carter. And thank you," she says right before she hangs up.

I don't need to ask her what she's thanking me for, I already know. But she doesn't need to thank me. I was telling the truth.

Less than twenty-four hours and I'll be picking her up. I can't wait.

9

JANIE

HALF MY CLOSET IS ON MY BED. I'VE GONE through everything, and nothing seems to be right. I've tried to remind myself that Carter is just a friend, and it doesn't really matter what I wear, but all day all I've thought about is him. I know I wish this was more than it is, but I'm not going to focus on that. Instead, I'm going to enjoy it while it lasts. I know he'll get tired of me probably sooner than not, so that's why I've decided to just enjoy it while I can.

I walk over to the mirror in my bedroom just as the doorbell rings. My father is downstairs, so I know he'll answer it, but I probably need to hurry. I look at my jeans and turn to the side. They're definitely tight but not so tight they're obscene. It's hot out, so I have on my blue tank top and I grab my lined flannel purple shirt off the bed. My hair's up, and I've already put on mascara and some lip gloss. At this point, it's the best it's going to get.

I all but run down the stairs, hoping that my dad is not too far into the interrogation that I know he's going to give Carter. "Hey, I'm ready," I say as I walk up to my dad, kiss him on the cheek, and walk past Carter to the front door.

"Honey, are you trying to rush Carter out of here? He looks like he's had a hard day. Let him rest a minute." My dad is smirking. I'm sure he knows what I'm trying to do.

For the first time since I've walked into the room, I look at Carter, and my stomach drops. "Carter, what's wrong? Are you okay?"

His hair is wet, like he's just freshly showered, but it's obvious he's tired. The lines in his face are defined more than they were when I saw him just two days ago, and he looks as if he's about dead on his feet.

"Yeah, I'm fine," he tells me before turning to my father. "Thank you for the offer of coffee, Blake, but I'm going to pass. I'll have Janie back this evening."

They shake hands, and I stand at the door until Carter walks up behind me. When his hand presses against my lower back and he opens the door, I walk out in front of him. I don't get far, though. I stop on the porch and watch as he limps out of the house. "Carter... I'm not going riding with you."

He puts his hand back on my waist. "Too late, sugar. No backing out now."

I shake my head. "No, I mean, you're obviously tired. You've been on a horse all day, and I know you're hurting. I'm not going to make you get back on a horse tonight."

"Janie, I've been looking forward to this all day. I already have dinner in the truck."

I swing my head to look at his truck and then back at him. "Okay, so here's an option. We can bring the food in and eat it here. We can watch television and just hang out."

"Are you afraid to be alone with me?" he asks.

"No! Of course not. I trust you completely, but I'm not going to risk you getting hurt worse than you are. You're obviously tired."

He reaches for my hand and pulls it up between us. His fingers wrap around mine, and my heart starts to race. Just from a simple touch, he has my body reacting to him. "Or another option, I take you out to my ranch. I mean, the house is not done, but I'd like you to see it. And there's nowhere to really sit, but..."

"I have chairs in the garage. I'll grab those." I start to walk over to the garage. They're right inside, and as soon as I grab them, he takes them from me. "Here. I got them."

I follow behind him, taking in his slight limp. I know he doesn't want me to notice it, but there's no avoiding it. "And I think I'll drive my car so you don't have to come back into town."

He loads two chairs into the back of his truck and then comes for me. "Nope. No way, not going to happen. I'm not going to worry about you driving back into town tonight. You're coming with me."

I do as he says but still argue with him. "So I'll just worry about you then when you have to drive all the way back home."

I get into the truck, and he pulls the

seatbelt securely around me and plugs it into place. "I'll be fine."

He's close, and I can feel his breath on my cheek. I look at him, taking him in, and examine him up close. There's a tiredness in his eyes, but there's something else too.

He stares back at me and licks his lips. "Friends," he mutters.

My eyes widen. "What?"

"Friends. That's what we agreed to. But I've never had a friend that I wanted to kiss like I want to kiss you."

I reach up and grab on to his forearm. His muscles cord under my palm. I shouldn't taunt him, and I'm not a flirt, but it comes out so easily. "Maybe we can be kissing friends."

He leans his forehead against mine. "I'd like that, Janie. I'd like that a lot."

He doesn't kiss me, though. He stands up almost rigidly and shuts the door before moving around to the driver's side. As soon as he's in, he backs out of the driveway and starts driving toward his ranch.

We talk about our days, and I tell him that I haven't heard back on any of my applications that I've submitted so far. The ride out to the ranch is quiet and peaceful. Neither one of us feels the need to fill the silence. He turns down a dirt road and drives about a half mile when his house comes into view.

"This is it," he says as he turns into the long driveway. I can hear the pride in his voice, and I turn in my seat to take it all in. The walls and roof are all up. It looks like the siding still needs to be completed, but I can already tell the house is going to be beautiful. There's a big wraparound porch that is almost finished, and when he stops in front of the big house, he leans on the steering wheel. "That's my favorite part."

I look out the front windshield and gasp. My hands go to my mouth. "Oh my gosh, Carter. It's beautiful. I've never seen anything like it." I reach for the door and stumble out before he can come around to help me. As if drawn toward the lake and mountain view, I walk to the edge of the property to the fencing. Carter walks up behind me. He doesn't touch me, but he doesn't have to. I can feel his heat as if he's all around me.

"This is just beautiful, Carter."

"Thank you."

I turn and look up at him. "Tell me all about it. What are you going to do on your ranch? Breed horses, cows? I know I sound dumb, but I want to know all about it."

He brushes a piece of hair off my face. "You could never sound dumb. It's a small ranch. I bought ten acres from Austin and his family." He points off to the side where the lake water ends and toward Jasper. "My acreage goes that way. I'm going to train horses. I've already hired a good hand. Chase Michael. He's great with horses, and I'm excited to get him started. Anyway, training horses is something I'm good at, and since I can't compete anymore, I thought this would be a good way for me to kind of stay in the game."

I clasp my hands under my chin excitedly. I can tell he's happy with his plans. "That's perfect. I bet you're good."

He shrugs, not wanting to brag, but I really want to know. "No, tell me. I want you to brag. Do you miss it?"

He nods instantly. "Yeah, I miss it. I think I always will, but now having this, well, it's like

OBSESSED COWBOY   85

I have something else to fill that void now. And yeah, I was good. I'm already booked out for training. As soon as the barn is finished"—he points out to the barn that looks complete from here—"I'll be able to get started."

"And Austin sold you this land, knowing he'd lose you on his ranch?" I ask, not understanding. I've heard the ladies talking at church about how hard it's been to find help on the local ranches. I can't believe Austin would willingly lose a rancher and a good one at that.

"Yeah, I was surprised too, but it was his idea. Austin and I are close; we have been for a long time. I worked on the ranch for his parents since I was fifteen and even while I was on the circuit. We're more like family. They sort of saved me in foster care."

I interrupt him. "I didn't know you were in foster care."

He nods. "Yep, I never knew my dad, and my mom left me when I was young." He stops for an instant and then continues. "I spend all my holidays with the Yates, and Mylie and Abby call me Uncle Carter," he says, talking about Austin and Millie's twin daughters.

"That's good, Carter. I'm glad that you have that... that you have a family."

He nods. "Yeah, my marriage didn't work out, but it obviously does for some people. Millie loves Austin and her kids. She'd never leave them."

I put my hand on his chest and curl my fingers into his shirt. He's telling me more than he realizes, I'm sure. "Most women don't leave, Carter."

He shrugs. "Yeah, I mean if they love someone, I mean really love them, they won't."

I move in closer to him and touch his chin so he looks down at me instead of over my head. "I don't know what happened between you and your ex-wife, but I don't believe your mom didn't love you. She may have been sick, overwhelmed, or maybe something happened, I don't know. But there's no way I could believe your mother didn't love you."

He shrugs like it's not a big deal, but I know it is. "Well, I'll never know. I heard she passed away a few years ago." He puts his hand on my shoulder. "Let's talk about something else. I didn't mean to get deep on you."

I reach up and cover his hand that's resting on my shoulder. "Okay, what do you want to talk about?"

He smirks. "How about us being kissing friends?"

I laugh, and a snort comes out. I cover my face, embarrassed.

"You snorted!" He starts to laugh, and I playfully smack him on the chest.

He catches my hand and brings it up to his shoulders. By this point, I'm laughing with him. "I don't think you're supposed to point it out."

He ducks his head so we're looking into each other's eyes. "It's cute."

I shake my head, not wanting to laugh in fear that I'll snort again. "No, it's definitely not cute."

He puts his large, rough hands on each side of my face. "I think it is."

I stop laughing then, entranced by the look on his face. "Are you going to kiss me?" I ask him and then blush, thinking how stupid that sounds.

He nods. "I want to."

I close my eyes and wait.

His voice is gruff. "Can I kiss you, Janie?"

I blink, opening my eyes. This is my out. I already know I'm in too deep with him, but I can't tell him no. "Yes, I hope you do."

He leans in slowly and presses his lips to mine. He takes his time, nibbling at my lip, pressing soft kisses to the corners of my lips. I remember the other night and open my mouth to him. He doesn't hesitate. He deepens the kiss as one hand slides around to the nape of my neck and the other one holds on to my ponytail. He pulls it backwards slowly, and I bend to his will, letting his tongue mate with mine.

We're so close, but I need him closer. I move against his body, and the friction pushes me further, sliding my body along his like a cat that wants to be petted. My nipples harden, and there's a tug in my lower belly, but I can't imagine stopping.

He leans me against the fence post and slides his leg between the two of mine. He's hard everywhere I'm soft, and I whimper at his demanding touch. His leg rises, and I moan loudly against his mouth. My thighs are trembling, and between my mound feels swollen and needy.

I should stop, I know I should, but he lifts his leg again, and there's an intense feeling that rocks through my whole entire body, and I freeze against him. Gasping, I pull away. My eyes are large and rounded, staring at him.

His eyes are dark and needy, his lips swollen from what we were just doing. "I'm sorry. We should stop."

But he doesn't back away, and he doesn't move his leg. He pushes it against me again, and my head falls back. "Oh my!" I moan.

He lifts my head, searching my face. "Are you okay? Do you want me to stop?"

"I can't have sex with you," I tell him, at least lucid enough to not completely forget my whole upbringing.

He studies me, and I know he sees the desire and longing. I can't hide that from him. "I can please you, Janie. I can do that, and we won't have sex."

Instantly, I shake my head. "I can't. I shouldn't."

He lowers his leg, and I miss it already. I

clutch on to his shirt and hold him close, fearful that he's going to push away from me. "I've never... I mean..."

He kisses my forehead, patiently waiting for me to finish, but I can't. He pulls back and asks, "You've never what?"

I look down at the button on his shirt. There's no way I can confess this to him and look him in the eye. "I've never had an orgasm."

He moans as if he's in pain. His breaths are coming in little pants as if he's out of breath. "Do you want one, Janie? Can I be the one to give it to you?"

I hesitate, and he continues. "Nothing else. I don't want anything in return. I just want to make you feel good."

I look around, and there's no house or animal in view, but that doesn't mean there isn't someone. "What if someone saw me?"

He pulls back, grabbing both of my hands. "I wouldn't do that to you. I wouldn't risk letting anyone see you. I can take you in the house; I want to show you anyway. You can think about it. You don't have to decide right now."

I release a breath, finally able to relax. It's too much pressure for right now, and I'm glad he's giving me an out. My body is still vibrating, and I hate the feeling when he steps back but at least he doesn't let go of my hand. "Do you want to eat? Are you hungry?"

I nod, and we walk back toward the house. The sun is still hot, so he points to the porch. "Head on up there, honey, and I'll grab the stuff."

I walk up the steps and feel bad after he makes three trips to bring everything up. "I can help you, ya know?"

He shakes his head and kisses my forehead as he puts the chairs on one end of the porch and then spreads out a blanket. "The first thing I'm buying is a table and chairs. I'm sorry you have to sit on the ground to eat."

I shake my head and sit down on the blanket as I pull out the items in the bags. "This is perfect. And I mean, how could anyone complain with that view?"

He sits down next to me and kicks his leg out. "Yum, is this from Red's?" I ask him, recognizing the labels on the packages.

"It is. I told Violet I was feeding you dinner, and she said she knew just the thing."

He shrugs like it's not a big deal, but I can't help asking, "You told Violet you were eating dinner with me?"

He grimaces defensively. "Is that a problem?"

I shake my head. "Not for me it's not. And Violet's not a gossip, but everyone else in Whiskey Run is. They're going to think something's going on with us... I mean, they're going to think we're dating or something."

10

CARTER

She has a point, and I know she does, but I hadn't thought about it. I've never lived my life worrying what people thought of me, but now, knowing Janie and who she is, I can see how it could be a bad thing. "I wasn't thinking about it. I'm sorry, Janie."

She lifts her chin. "You don't have to apologize to me. I'm sure everyone was already talking anyway since you escorted me to church the other night. I can handle what people say about me. I just don't want it to mess with you or for you to think I'm spreading rumors about us or anything."

I lean forward. "Wait. You're telling me you're worried about me?"

She shrugs like it's no big deal and continues to take out the containers. I put my hand on hers to stop her. "You're worried about me?"

Her shoulders drop, and she tilts her head to the side. "Is that so hard to believe? I don't want you stressing about this." She gestures between the two of us. "I know where you stand, and you've told me your intentions. I just don't want you feeling bad or pressured or anything."

I put my hand on her thigh and squeeze. "You're something else, Janie, but you don't have to worry about me. I can handle it, and gossip doesn't bother me. I just ignore it."

She nods. "Good to know."

She smiles and then gestures to the bag between us. "Now, if you don't mind, I'm pretty sure that Violet packed me a slice of apple cinnamon Blaze cake."

I laugh. "Well, I'm definitely not going to get between a woman and her apple cinnamon Blaze cake."

I sit back as she finishes unpacking the bag. I grab the drinks out of the cooler and can't seem to take my eyes off Janie. She's nothing like I expected, but everything I've ever dreamed of. I wish I'd met her sooner, before my life went to shit and I got this hardened heart. I have a feeling that she would have handled it a lot better than my ex-wife did.

We talk and eat for what seems like only minutes, but when dusk starts to set in and there's only about another half hour of daylight, I realize it's been hours. We've moved to the chairs, and I moved close so that I could hold her hand between us. I keep telling myself that we're going to be friends, and that's all this can be, but my heart and my body keep betraying me. It's like I can't be close to her and not touch her.

"Well, I should probably get you back into town."

She looks startled. "Really? I thought you were going to show me the inside of the house."

I shake my head. I know if I take her inside, I'm going to continue what we started earlier. "No, I don't think that's a good idea, Janie. I think I probably need to take you home."

She shrugs and gets up to start packing

things away. But she wasn't quick enough. I can see the hurt in her eyes, and that's the last thing I wanted to do. I throw the chairs in the back of the truck and meet her back up on the porch. I stop when I'm right in front of her. "Janie, honey."

"Yeah?" she answers without looking at me.

"Look at me."

She does, but her face is guarded. "What are you thinking right now?"

She shrugs. "Nothing."

She tries to step around me, but I put my hands on her shoulders to stop her. "Talk to me."

She blinks. "What did I do wrong?"

I tighten my hold on her. "You didn't do anything wrong."

She puts her hand on her hip and almost sassily asks me, "Well, then why wouldn't you want to show me your house? I know you're proud of it. I can hear it in your voice just when you talk about it here. I want to see it."

I move my hands to her neck. "Because if I take you inside, I'm going to finish what I started earlier. I want to hear you moaning my name."

Her eyes are big, but she doesn't say a thing. I know I'm moving too fast for her. I release her, and when I do, she turns and walks into the house. She looks over her shoulder at me as she walks across the threshold. She's smiling, and even from here I can see the excitement on her face.

I still my hands together, fighting the urge to chase after her and ravage her. *Just make her come, Carter. That's it. Make this night memorable for her, but don't make her regret it.*

With a plan in mind, I walk in after her. She holds her hand out to me, and I grab on to it. "Show me," she asks.

I nod and take her through the house, showing her every room and what the plans are for it. She asks questions, letting me know that she's really interested. I ask her opinion on things, and she gives me ideas that I'd never thought of. When we get to the bedroom, she sees the already framed mattress in the center of the room. "Carter, are you sleeping here?"

I shrug. "It's not a big deal. Just

sometimes." I can feel my face heat. "I'm excited to move in."

She looks at me with so much understanding and warmth. "I'm excited for you."

I pull her to me, and her hands go to my waist. "Do you know what I'm really excited about?"

She looks at me questioningly.

"Kissing you. I want to kiss you again."

Her fingers tighten and dig into my skin. "I want that too."

I don't doubt her. I can hear the yearning in her voice, and when she tilts her head up to me, there's no holding back. I kiss her, hard and fast. The temptation of sitting with her the last few hours, getting to know her and knowing that I don't deserve her but my heart is racing to have her, I don't hold back. I put everything I have into that kiss. She groans against me, and I pull back, not wanting to hurt her or push her too far.

Her lips are swollen. "Can you... I mean will you... I mean, I want you to give me my first orgasm. I promised myself I'd save myself for marriage, but I can't deny that I want—no, I need this with you. Please?"

I pick her up, and she laughs. "Carter, put me down. I'm too heavy."

I swat her ass with my hand and then squeeze it. "You're not either. You're just right," I tell her as I lay her down on the bed. Her breasts are high, peeking out the top of her tank top, and I would give anything to suckle them, but I don't want to push her. "Tell me what you want. Exactly, Janie. I don't want to mess this up or for you to regret it."

"I want you to make me feel like you did earlier, Carter. I was so close. I want to feel it again."

"Where?" I all but grunt the word at her. "Where do you want me to touch you?"

She grabs my hand and while looking straight into my eyes and brings my hand down between her legs. She presses my fingers into the apex of her thighs. Her voice is throaty. "Here. I want you to touch me here."

I rub her there, feeling the heat of her through her jeans. "Can I go under your clothes? I want to touch you with nothing between us."

She nods. "I trust you."

I take a deep breath and unbutton her jeans. I lower the zipper, and it's the only sound in the room besides our heavy breathing. I put a hand at each side of her hip and pull her pants down to her thighs. She kicks her boots off, so I pull them all the way down and let them fall to the floor. She's still in her white panties, and the sight of her has my cock hard and thick between my legs. I ignore it, though. This is not about me. It's all about her.

There's a wet patch, showing me how turned on she is right now. I want to lick and taste her, but I know one taste won't be enough.

"I'm going to pull these down, okay?" I ask her as I put a finger on the hips of her panties.

She clears her throat and nods, but that's not good enough. "Tell me it's okay. Tell me you want this."

She reaches for me, touching the hand at her right hip. "I want this, Carter. I want it with you."

I pull her panties down and let them fall to

the floor. She has a small patch of hair, and I hold in my groan when she parts her legs. Her pink pussy is glistening, even in the low light. I can smell her desire, and it surrounds me, pulling me in. I run my hands up her thighs, and she lifts her body up off the bed like an electric charge went through her. She blushes, and I smile, loving that her body is reacting like this to me.

"You need this, don't you, baby? You don't just want it, you need it."

She mewls low in her throat. "Yes."

I push her thighs apart with one hand and cover her mound with my other. Her hips buck, and I settle myself down between her legs. I stroke my finger through her wet, swollen slit. She coats my finger, and because I can't help myself, I pull it from her folds and put it in my mouth. "Mmmm," I groan, tasting her.

She lifts up on her elbows, watching me. "Did you—? Is that—?"

I lick my lips. "Did I just lick your cream off my finger? Yes, I did."

She takes a shuddering breath and watches me as I stroke my thumb through her folds again. I press against her nub and watch her head fall back. I circle her clit, harder, softer and then harder again. She's lifting her hips, pushing herself against me. When she's close, I pull back and lick my finger again.

Her head snaps back, her eyes wide. "Why? Why'd you stop?"

"Because I wanted to taste you. I want you on my tongue."

"You mean..." she starts and stops again.

I move closer, and I know she can feel my heavy breath on her channel. "I mean, I want to put my mouth on you. I want you to come in my mouth."

She nods, her eyes hooded. She's already so far gone, I'm afraid she'll agree to anything at this point.

"Say it, Janie."

When she doesn't answer, I swat her hip. "Say it. I need to hear you say it out loud."

She groans. "I want you to put your mouth on me."

I almost dive in but stop at the last minute. "Tell me you're not going to regret this. I won't be able to live with myself if I hurt you."

She reaches up and runs her hands through my hair. "I won't regret it."

There's no stopping me then. I lean in and suction my mouth to her. I slide my tongue through her wet, needy sex. When I have her juices in my mouth and dripping down my chin, I wrap my tongue around her swollen clit and don't stop until she's bucking underneath me and finally screams out the orgasm, saying my name and filling the room with her cries.

Even after she's completely satisfied, and her body's limp underneath me, I still don't stop. I could do this all night. When she groans, I rest my head on her lower belly, the scent of her all over me. It's almost completely dark, and I know I need to get her home.

I groan as I get up. My cock is angry, hard, and thick between my legs. I can't do anything about it now, but I'm sure I'll be coming tonight with Janie's name on my lips.

"You okay?" I ask her.

She's beautiful, lying there, completely open to me. I wish I could bare my cock and dive right in. I don't think she'd stop me, but I know I couldn't do that to her. I grab her panties and start to put them on, and she gets up to help me. We're both quiet as we gather everything up and I help her to the truck. She puts on her seatbelt herself, and I walk around quickly. She's looking straight ahead, not saying anything. I don't know if she's mad, upset or what, but something's not right.

She's quiet, and I fear that she's starting to regret what we just did. "Are you okay?" I ask her again.

I can't see her face when she says, "Yes, I'm good."

In my head, I'm trying to think of ways to apologize to her and to tell her I'm sorry, but I can't even begin to do so. There's no way I could be sorry for what just happened between us. I'm about to tell her just that when her phone rings.

She answers it hurriedly, as if she can't wait to talk to someone else besides me. "Hello?"

I turn down the music in the truck, and it's easy to hear the conversation that is taking place.

"Hi Janie. This is Emery at Sugar Glaze Bakery."

Janie's voice perks up. "Oh, hi, Emery."

"Hi. I'm sorry for calling you so late, it's been a busy day. I just wanted to call and offer you the job. It's the starting pay we talked about, and you'd work primarily nights and Saturdays. I can honor your request to be off on Sundays. We can get the training going as soon as you can start."

Janie seems excited and almost bounces in her seat. "Tomorrow. I can start tomorrow."

Emery, or whatever her name is, can hear the excitement in her voice too, because she laughs. "That's great, Janie. I look forward to seeing you. About 1 p.m. tomorrow?"

"That's great. I'll be there." Janie's about to hang up when Emery says, "Oh yeah, Janie?"

"Yeah?"

Emery's voice drops a little like she's embarrassed or something. "My brother, Jamison, said he graduated with you. Anyway, I told him I was hiring you and hoped you took the job... well, anyway, he told me to tell you hi and he looked forward to seeing you this week."

Janie pauses, and I can feel her glance over

at me. My hands tighten on the steering wheel. Son of a bitch. I knew she wouldn't be back in town long before men started lining up at her door. Janie clears her throat. "Yeah, I remember Jamison. He was always nice to me. I look forward to seeing him too."

They hang up, and I stew the rest of the way into town. Did she just make a date with someone else right in front of me? The need to punch something is almost overwhelming.

I pull into her driveway, get out, and help her out of the truck. I grab her chairs and carry them to the garage while she opens the door for me. I put them down where they were and walk out into the driveway.

She's looking up at me like she's filled with regret. It's all too much. I have this obsessive need to have her, to stake my claim on her right now, but I know I can't. Guilt claims me. "Are you okay?" I ask her for the third time.

She nods but doesn't say anything else.

"Congratulations on your job," I tell her.

She nods. "Yeah, I'm excited about it. But look, I went to school with Jamison—"

I cut her off. "It's nothing, Janie. We're

friends, right? I can't tell you who you can and who you can't talk to."

She nods, and I know I need to get out of here. I have to before I do something stupid and tell her that she's mine and she can't go out with another man. I'm the one that made the decision that we should be friends. And I know she's nothing like my ex-wife, but can I trust her to not get tired of me and leave? She's so young, she probably doesn't have any idea what she wants.

"I have to go. Early morning," I tell her as I lean in and kiss her on the forehead.

I turn before I talk myself out of it. I sit in the truck until I see her disappear into the house. Even then, I sit here and wonder what the hell I'm doing. I shouldn't leave it like this. I can't. But hearing how excited she was about the job and knowing how young she is, I know I can't ruin this for her. She needs to live her life and figure out what she wants.

11

JANIE

It's been three days since I've heard from Carter. I never thought he'd be this way, but obviously I know nothing. Maybe he just wanted to prove that he could get into the pants of the preacher's daughter. I blush just thinking about it. It's all I've thought about since that night.

I'm loving my job. I'm really enjoying the marketing part, but more than anything, I'm loving learning to bake. Every day I've brought home new treats I've made for my father, and he loves them. He knows something's up with me, but I'm glad he hasn't asked me about it. He's only offered to listen if I wanted to talk.

My first night at Sugar Glaze, two of the girls were going to The Whiskey Whistler. I went, and it was my first time in a bar. I was expecting to get looks or disappointing stares, but I didn't. But also, I didn't see anyone from my father's congregation either.

"So are you in tonight?" Tara asks me on my third night at Sugar Glaze.

"In for what?" I ask her as I start to count the till. She's been training me on closing, and she's been so much fun.

"For The Whistler. I'm meeting April, and I thought you'd like to go."

I shake my head. "No, I'd better not."

Tara, who has been super sweet to me, leans across the counter. "You have to get over him."

Confused, I ask her. "Who?"

She crosses her arms on her chest. "Carter Grant. I mean he's hot, I'll give you that. But you can't just mope around. He's not really a settling down kind of guy and—"

"Wait!" I stop trying to count the till and hold my hand up. "What are you talking about? Carter and I weren't dating."

She looks at me like she doesn't believe me. "Really? Everyone... I mean—"

"No, what do you mean everyone... is everyone saying that Carter broke up with me?"

She starts to look uneasy, and I'm sure it's because my voice is raised. She shrugs her shoulders. "It was all over town that you were seeing each other, and well, now you're not. People are just saying that they feel sorry for you."

I gasp. "Feel sorry for me?"

I roll my eyes. The joys of living in a small town. My mind starts to go a mile a minute. Is that why he hasn't called? Did he think that I planned this—that I told everyone he broke up with me? I put my hand to my head. "Oh my God, are people saying things to him?"

She shrugs again. "I don't know. I heard over at Red's Diner earlier that he hadn't been in town. They're talking about when he does they're going to say something, though."

I grab on to her hand. "No! They can't do that. We weren't dating. We're just friends," I tell her, even though just saying the words makes me feel not right.

She shrugs. "Well, if that's true, I feel sorry for Carter. I'm sure people are going to say something to him. You're sort of the sweetheart of Whiskey Run. Everyone loves you and wants to look out for you."

I cover my face and start to pace. *How do I fix this? How do I fix this?* I ask myself. A thought pops into mind, and I whirl on Tara. "Yes, I'm going with you tonight. Let's finish up so I can get ready." I look down at my pink Sugar Glaze T-shirt and jeans. "I can't go like this."

"I have a shirt you can wear."

I shake my head. "I'm sure it won't fit."

She jumps up and down. "No, it will fit perfectly. Now let's get going."

We finish cleaning up and doing the closing procedures. Everything runs smoothly, and I feel like I've got a good handle on things. When we're done, we go into the bathroom and both start to get ready. I didn't really have close girlfriends growing up, so when Tara offers to do my hair and makeup, I sit back on the stool and let her do it. When she's done, I can't stop staring at myself in the mirror. I look like a completely different person. I don't look anything like Janie Bradshaw, preacher's daughter.

"And for the finishing touch, here you go."

I hold out my hand, and Tara puts a shirt in it. I hold it up, and it has quite a bit less of material than I'm used to. "I don't know..."

"Put it on."

I look at her hesitatingly and she says, "Trust me?"

I nod and pull my pink T-shirt off and then put on her black T-shirt. It's sleeveless and has holes cut across the shoulders and chest. It's not showing anything that I wouldn't be showing in a tank top, but the style is definitely new for me. "I don't know. Are you sure about this?"

She nods. "You look great."

I look in the mirror again, and I have to agree with her. It's definitely not a look I can pull off around town, but I can wear it at the Whiskey Whistler and fit right in. I blow out a breath. "All right, let's go before I change my mind."

We walk down the block and into the Whiskey Whistler, I wave at Malcolm. He's the owner of the bar, and he warned me the first night I was here that if my dad got upset with him about me being here, then I needed to not come. I didn't argue with him. I try to stay low key, and I wouldn't want to harm any business.

Tonight, I'm on a mission, though. Even though I don't want to, I'm going to talk to other men and even try to flirt. It's not going to be fun, and I'm probably going to feel guilty, but it's necessary. I can't have all of Whiskey Run gossiping about Carter breaking my heart.

***

Carter

I HAVEN'T SEEN Janie in three days. I haven't even talked to her since the night I dropped her off at her house. I haven't been able to stop thinking of her, though. I spent the night at my house after I dropped her off and went to the Yates Ranch at five a.m. the next morning for work. I was about to start on the morning feed when Austin came and found me. "I need you to go to Kentucky."

I looked at him in shock. It was the worst

time ever for me to leave Whiskey Run. I hadn't been able to stop thinking about Janie, and now I had to worry about some man named Jamison that obviously remembered her from years ago. No, I didn't want to go out of town.

But I wasn't in a place to tell him no. I was the only one that could take the horse trailer and pick up the injured and hurt thoroughbreds. I could handle those kinds of horses better than anyone. So I did my job and drove straight to Kentucky. When I got there, I found out that there were more horses coming, and so instead of driving back and forth, I'd stayed two nights so I could make it in one trip.

I thought of Janie the whole time. How could I not? I was right; one taste of her was not enough. I'm driven with the need to have her and the need to give her space and make sure she knows what she wants.

I got back to the ranch a few hours ago. I unloaded the horses, showered, and headed straight into town. I knew I should probably sleep, but there's no way I could have gone another night without seeing her.

I pull into her father's driveway and jog up to the front door. I hit the doorbell and then knock too. I know I sound anxious, probably because I am.

Her father opens the door. "Oh, hey, Carter. How's it going?"

I nod. "Good, sir. Can I speak to Janie?"

He opens the door farther. "I'm sorry. She's not here."

I run my hand through my hair. "Oh, is she still at work?"

He shakes his head. "No, she got off a little while ago. She was going to the Whistler with some of her new friends."

"The Whistler? You mean the bar?"

He shrugs and nods his head. "Yes, I'm afraid so. She doesn't drink, and I have to let her live her own life. She knows right from wrong."

The whole speech makes me think that he's trying to remind himself instead of me. I thank him and hightail it back to my truck. I can't believe she's at a bar. I've been worried this whole time about her employer's brother, and now I know I should be worrying about every man that hangs out at the Whistler. And they're drinking too. Janie's so innocent; she has no idea what she's gotten herself into.

I drive toward the bar and park on the street a block away. I don't waste any time. I run down the block but then stop right outside the doors. I take three deep, calming breaths. I can't run in there and embarrass her. This is Whiskey Run, and I don't want to upset her. I keep telling myself that over and over as I calmly walk in and take a seat at the bar. My back is to the dance floor and all the tables.

"How you doing, Carter?"

I look at the man beside me. I didn't even realize it when I sat down, but my friend Garrett is sitting drinking a whiskey. "I'm good. How've you been? How's Kaylee?" I ask him, referring to his longtime best friend. I'm trying to pay attention, but also looking in the mirror over the bar to see if I can find Janie.

"She's doing well and coming into town next weekend to visit her dad and we have plans to grab dinner and catch up."

"That's good, man," I tell him.

"How's the new ranch coming, Carter?"

I look to my other side, and Ledger is sitting there. I chuckle. "What's up, rich boy?"

He laughs good naturedly. "Not much, just working."

I nod. "Me too. The ranch is coming along fine."

Malcolm spots me and just by the guilty look on his face, my fists clinch and I slam it on the bar top. "Where is she, Malcolm?"

HE POINTS behind me and I see her in the corner dancing with another man. I jump out of my seat and can feel the rage coming through my veins. I tell the two men beside me that I gotta go and stalk over to Janie.

It's a fast song, but the person she's dancing with obviously doesn't care because he's holding her like it's a slow one. Everyone in the bar stops, and the only sound is the country song playing on the juke box. I can feel everyone's eyes on me, but I stopped giving shits about one minute ago when I saw her in the arms of another man.

I stride toward Janie, glaring at the man with her. "Get your hands off her, Pete."

Pete puts his hands up and backs off.

Janie puts her hand on her hip. "Really,

Carter? You can't tell me who I can dance with."

My jaw tightens, and my fists clench at my sides. "Oh yes, I can."

The whole room is staring at us. Janie walks up to me and points a finger in my chest. "You don't want me. You just don't want anyone else to have me. Well, I'm not playing that game anymore."

"There's no game, Janie. You're mine. You have been since I first laid eyes on you."

Janie opens her mouth to argue, but she doesn't get a chance. I pick her up, swinging her over my shoulder. With a hand on her ass, I hold her in place and stalk out the door. It will be all over town by tomorrow, but I don't care. I'm tired of playing it safe. I put her down when we get out the door. She tries to walk off, toward the bakery, but I grab her hand and walk her back to my truck. I put her in and put the seatbelt on.

"My car..." she says, pointing down the block.

"You can get it tomorrow," I tell her. I'm mad. I'm fuming mad. I can't get the image of Peter's hands on her out of my mind. No one should be able to touch her. No one but me.

I get in the driver's seat and slam the door. "The whole damn town..." I start, but she interrupts me.

"I know, Carter. I know. They all think you broke up with me and broke my heart. I never said a thing to anyone. I know we're friends. I didn't expect the town to turn on you. That's why I was at the bar tonight. I wanted people to think I was okay... I didn't want anyone mad at you."

I stop then and stare at her with my mouth hanging open. "Wait... you did that for me? You were protecting me?"

She rolls her eyes. "Well, yeah. You're a good man, Carter. It's not your fault that you don't like me. You didn't do anything wrong."

I shake my head, still wanting to make things clear. "You didn't want to dance with Peter?"

She blanches. "No, and I told him I wasn't interested in anything other than a dance."

I sit back in my seat, stunned. Was I really just going to give her up and let her decide what she wants? After the scene I made tonight, she no longer has that choice. I grabbed the preacher's daughter's ass right in front of everyone. I claimed her as mine. How could I be so stupid to think I could just let her go?

I put the truck into gear and take off, spinning tires as I pull out of the spot. Janie puts her hand on the dash, and she's talking to me, asking me if I'm okay. Guilt eats at me.

I don't say a word. As soon as I get to her house, I help her out of the truck. "Thanks for the ride," she says and sounds almost in tears.

I don't say a word. I follow behind her and up the steps to her porch. She turns when she realizes I'm right behind her. "Carter, what are you doing?"

"I need to talk to your dad."

She wraps her arms around her waist. "What? You're telling on me? He knows I was at the bar."

I clench my teeth. "I need to talk to your dad."

As soon as I get the words out, Pastor Blake opens the door. "Is everything okay?"

Janie stomps up the stairs. "Yeah, Dad. I'm going to bed. Carter needs to talk to you."

Pastor Blake waves me into the living room. "Have a seat, son."

I sit down but then pop right back up. I pace along the carpet and stop suddenly. "I've tried to be a good man."

He nods, and I continue. "I know I've messed up. I know I have, but I'm trying to be a better man."

He still doesn't say anything, but at least he doesn't look mad. He's lying back in his recliner, watching me as I pace back and forth. "Okay, well, what I need to talk to you about is... well, I'd like to marry your daughter."

Pastor Blake sits up higher in his chair. "You want to marry my daughter. You want to marry Janie," he says, as if to clarify.

I nod. "Yes, I know she deserves better than me. I know that I can't give her everything she deserves, but I'm going to live every day trying to be a better man, a man that she deserves and that one day she loves."

He tilts his head to the side, and I can tell he's thinking. He's always been a patient man, and I wait for the question that I can see brewing in his head. "What the rush?"

I sit down on the chair across from him

and lean forward. "Because I can't go one more day and not know she's mine. She brings me so much peace of mind, she makes me laugh, hell—I mean heck, sorry—she makes me happy. I can't imagine not being with her, sir."

He crosses his arms over his chest. "Well, that's all well and good, son. But do you love her?"

I put my hand to my chest and give him an honest and heartfelt answer. All I can do is hope he approves.

12

JANIE

I HAVE MY HEAD TUCKED AGAINST MY PILLOW, trying to quiet the sobbing tears. I should have made Carter talk to me, but I didn't. So here I am, crying and sobbing because I did what I said I wouldn't do. I fell in love with him. He told me, he made it perfectly clear what I could expect from him, and I done screwed it up.

Knock. Knock.

"Go away, Dad. I'm fine. I'll talk to you in the morning."

The door opens, and I roll onto my side away from the door. My dad worries about me anyway; he doesn't need to see me like this. "I said I'm fine."

"I'm not leaving until I talk to you, Janie."

I gasp and jump up to a sitting position on my bed. "Carter! What are you doing in here?"

He kneels down on the floor next to my bed. His hands go to my thighs. Just that simple touch has my body tingling.

He touches my chin and brings it up to look at my face. He wipes the tears from my eyes and searches my face. "We're getting married."

I rear back. There's nothing he could have said that would have shocked me more. "Married?"

He nods. "Yes, we're getting married on Sunday. I already talked to your dad, and he gave us his blessing and agreed to perform the ceremony."

I shake my head. It's like a dream come true, but almost in the same thought, my stomach plummets. I know why he's doing this. He's trying to save my reputation... or maybe his, I don't know. I push myself up and stand by the open door. "I'm sorry, Carter. But I can't marry you."

He jumps to his feet, his eyes flashing and

jaw clenching. "You're going to marry me, Janie Bradshaw."

I cross my arms over my chest protectively. I would give anything to say yes. Anything at all, but watching him, he's not happy about this. It's obvious he's doing this because he has to. "I'm sorry, Carter. I can't marry you."

He pulls me to him, pushing his lips against mine. His kiss is ravaging, and I know I should save myself and push him away, but I can't. I love the feel of him against me. I've never felt safer and even more loved than I do right now... but that couldn't be further from the truth. He doesn't love me.

I pull away, panting. "You can keep kissing me, but I'm not going to marry you, Carter."

He stomps his foot and grips my shoulders. "You said it yourself, Janie. You said that the town hates me for breaking your heart. I won't be able to show my face here again. How can I start my own ranch in a town where people don't trust me? Now listen, I know I got us into this, and I know that you can do better than me, but I need you to marry me, Janie."

He takes a deep breath, and his chest expands against mine. "I'll have all the paperwork taken care of. Be at the church on Sunday at three."

He walks to my open door and stops and turns toward me. "And Janie, don't think about leaving. I'll find you."

He walks away, and only when I hear the front door slam a few seconds later do I let out a breath. How can I do this? How can I marry someone that is not capable of love?

A few seconds later, my dad comes to my door. "Everything okay?"

I nod. I blush just talking about it. I've never even had a real boyfriend, and now here I am talking about getting married. "Yeah, did you hear that Carter wants to marry me?"

My dad laughs. "Yeah, but the way he worded it, he's marrying you."

I go over and sit on my bed. "Dad, how can I marry him? He doesn't love me. He may never love me."

My dad's forehead creases in confusion. "Did he tell you that?"

I shake my head. "He didn't have to. When we went out, he said that he thought we should just be friends. I know his ex-wife did a number on him, but can I really marry someone and not know what the future holds?"

My dad sits on the bed beside me and takes my hand. "I've known Carter Grant for many years. I don't know if you know a lot of his story since he's older than you, but at one time, he was in foster care. His parents were nowhere to be found. The Yates took him in, and he was around fifteen at the time. He worked that ranch like it was his own. And then at one point he was married. She left him when he wasn't getting his own ranch fast enough. She wasn't made for ranch life. I saw it in his eyes when he had no family, I saw it in his eyes when his wife left him, and I see the same thing now. He just needs somewhere where he feels safe. He needs someone to love him as he is. If you feel that way about him, then you marry him. If you don't, then you tell him no and I'll stand by you when you do it. I just want you happy, Janie."

"I think I could be happy with Carter. I love him," I confess, even though my heart's breaking in two right now.

He nods and stands up. "Well, if you love

him, then your decision is made. The rest will fall into place, honey."

I look at the man that I've looked up to my whole life. He's helped people through marriages, divorces, births, deaths, and more. He's never once led someone wrong or told them something just because they wanted to hear it. He's honest and heartfelt, and knowing that he has my back makes all the difference in the world. "I love you, Dad."

"I love you too, sweetie."

I fall back on my bed. I can't believe I'm getting married in three days.

13

CARTER

ALL I WANT TO DO IS MAKE HER HAPPY, BUT somehow I've seemed to do the exact opposite. We got married earlier in her father's church, with just a few close friends in attendance. She looked breathtaking and beautiful in her white gown, and watching her as she walked down the aisle, I felt like I was going crazy because it felt like she wasn't going fast enough.

The ceremony was over quickly, and her friends at Sugar Glaze surprised us with a cake reception afterwards in the church dining hall. Everything was perfect, except for the fact that Janie seems miserable.

I made reservations for three nights at a hotel in Jasper. It's nothing exotic, and I wish I could take her somewhere better, but with the new horses at the Yates Ranch and getting our ranch set up, I couldn't take any more time off.

"Are you okay?" I ask her for the third time.

The drive to Jasper is only an hour, but the silence in the truck makes it seem so much longer. She's changed into a simple white summer dress, and it makes her look even more innocent. Again, for the third time, she says, "I'm fine."

We check into the hotel. "Are you hungry?" I ask her, pointing at the restaurant.

She nods, and I ask the bellman to take our bags to our room. I hold her hand and walk with her to the restaurant. I'm not hungry and feel like I can't eat a thing. I've been on edge since I put a ring on her finger this afternoon. The need to claim her is almost too much to bear.

We eat our meal. I barely touch the steak, and she barely touches her salad. The longer she's quiet, the more guilty I feel. I pushed her into this. Throwing it in her face that the town hates me and it'll ruin my reputation. I don't care about that; I panicked, and I had to have her. But now I'm wondering if I went about it the wrong way.

We get up to the room, and I can tell she needs some time to herself. I run the bath for her, dropping in bath salts. When it's full, I walk out into the bedroom. "I ran you a bath so you can relax."

She rises from the edge of the bed and nods her head. She's so beautiful. But it's more than that. She's standing before me with my ring on her finger, and I want her so badly. I want to take her, claim her as mine, and make her promise that she'll never leave me. The urge is so much, I'm almost afraid I won't be able to hold back and give her the first time she deserves.

I grab the key card off the dresser and walk toward the door. I can't stay in this room, knowing she's naked in the next room.

"Where are you going?" she asks.

I don't turn and look at her because I'm afraid if I do, I won't be able to leave. "Down to the bar."

I slam the door behind me, and instead of going to the elevator, I walk down the hall to the stairwell. I need the exercise. I need to do something to work off some of this energy that is raging through my body.

Two hours later, I feel that I have some control over myself. I didn't drink, but I did go to the weight room and worked out for the two hours. I pushed myself harder than I have in a long time, and I'm already feeling it in my leg.

I open the door to the hotel room, and the lights are off. She's lying as far to one side of the bed as she can get, and I go straight to the bathroom. I shower quickly, and then I slide under the cover in nothing but my underwear. I'm used to sleeping nude, but I don't want to freak her out.

I lie flat on my back, trying to listen to her breathing.

Her voice is low in the quiet room. "I think we should get an annulment."

"No," I answer her quickly. There's no way I can let her go. I can't.

She starts to cry, and my heart breaks. I told her I wouldn't hurt her, and look what I'm doing to her. I roll to my side. "Don't cry, Janie. Is it really that bad being married to me?"

"I can't do this, Carter. I can't be in a marriage where you feel trapped."

I reach for her, but she pulls even farther away from me. "You didn't trap me."

She sniffles, and a sob breaks free. "My dad said that since I loved you it would work out, you'll come around but..."

I lean up in bed and hover over top of her. "What did you say?"

She sniffles again. "My dad said..."

"No, not that. The part where you love me."

She covers her face with her arm. "I love you, Carter. You know I do. You warned me not to. You wanted to be friends, and I messed it up. The people of Whiskey Run ruined it, making you feel like you had to marry me."

I lean down and pull her arm away from her face. "No, they didn't ruin anything. I used them as an excuse. I didn't think you wanted to marry me, so I told you that so you'd feel like you had to marry me. I trapped you, Janie."

She blinks, looking up at me. There's a small light from the bathroom still on, and it gives some lighting to the room. Enough for

me to make out the look on her face. She's
staring at me in wonder. "You did? Why? Why
would you do that?"

I cup her jaw. "Because I love you.
Because I don't ever want another man's
hands on you. Because I wanted you to be
my wife and one day for you to have my
babies."

She leans toward me. "You do? But I
thought..."

"I was stupid, Janie. I love you. Please tell
me that you'll stay married to me. I'll work
every day to be the man you deserve. I won't
ever go out on you, and I'll always be here to
hold you and be here for you."

She dives across the bed, and I roll to my
back with her on top of me. "Yes, yes, a
thousand times, yes. I love you, Carter. You're
already the man I deserve. You're the best
man."

She kisses me, and it's urgent and filled
with need. I waste no time in pulling her gown
over her head. She's next to me in only her
panties, and I make fast work of getting them
off too. When I kick off my own and feel her
curvy naked body completely pressed against

mine, I can't hold back any longer. "I need you, Janie."

She nods. Her head is against my neck, and she kisses me there before whispering, "I need you too. Please don't make me wait any longer."

I pull back, trying to keep my senses. "I have condoms in my suitcase."

She stares at me, her face red and flushed. "Do you want to use them?"

I shake my head instantly. "No, I've dreamed of being inside you with nothing between us. But I don't want to make that decision on my own. You could get pregnant the first time even. I don't want to push you before you're ready."

Her eyes light up when I say pregnant, and just the image of her round with my babies in her belly makes my cock even harder. "I don't want anything between us either."

I groan as precum leaks from my cock.

I reach between us, stroking my finger through her sweet honey channel. "I need you wet, baby. I don't want to hurt you."

She grunts, and she's already soaked, ready for me. I roll onto my back and pull her on top of me. I stroke my hands up her waist and cup her heavy breasts as I lean up, my cock gliding along her bottom. I suckle her breast as her hands hold on to the back of my head, holding me to her.

I've coated her with my precum, and I know I have to get in her or it's going to be over before it even starts.

I lie back. "I don't want to hurt you. This time, I want you on top. You control it all, Janie. You can do anything you want."

She nods and reaches between us, wrapping her hand firmly around my cock. Her eyes widen, and I know she's shocked by the girth, but I just keep repeating to myself, *Don't hurt her, don't hurt her.*

"That's it, baby, put me inside you."

She raises up and puts me at her entrance. With just the tip in, I can already tell she's going to strangle my cock. She slides down slowly, and it's hell and heaven on earth at the same time. After only a few inches in, she stops, and I know I'm up against the tiny piece of skin that is keeping me from completely claiming her. I reach between us and put my finger on her clit. It's swollen, and I work across it, trying to take her focus off the pain I know she's about to feel. Her hips start to buck. "That's good, baby. Keep doing that, and when you come, when you feel your orgasm hit, I need you to slide down on me and take me all in."

She shakes her head side to side. "No, I want you to come too."

I smile. "Don't you worry about me. I'll come, baby. There's no doubt about it.'

She nods, and I put more pressure on her clit. She's shaking over top of me, and I know it's going to be soon. She starts to jerk, and I grab on to her hips and slam her down on my cock. Her eyes pop open, but she doesn't stop; she keeps rocking on my cock as I shoot rope after rope of cum deep inside her. When she stops moving, she falls down to my chest. I hold on to her and try to commit it all to memory. I don't ever want to forget this moment ever. I've claimed my wife... and I'm keeping her.

EPILOGUE

JANIE

Two Years Later

"LET'S GO SEE DADDY. YOU WANT TO?" I ASK our son.

The little boy that is the spitting image of his father nods and lifts his arms up, wanting me to carry him. I lift him up and put him on my hip.

I pick up the slice of pie on the counter and walk outside. I'm still doing the social media for the bakery, and I've added a few other clients to my list in the past year.

I walk out of the house, and just like every other time I look at it, I'm in awe. The ranch is done, and it's everything I'd imagined. The night Carter brought me here, he described it to me perfectly, and it's exactly the ranch he described. I walk toward the barn and stop next to the corral where Carter is training one of the new horses. There are a few cowboys standing to the side, and they all tip their hats to me, but none of them look my way long. Carter has pretty much put the word out that he doesn't appreciate anyone looking at me, and I understand he's protective. I act like it bothers me, but secretly I love his obsessive ways.

He rides over to us. "Hey, honey. Hey, CJ."

CJ holds his hands out for Carter to pick him up, but he shakes his head. "Not on this horse, buddy. We're still breaking him in. But I'll take you out on Stallion later."

CJ is only a little over a year old, but he acts like he understands every word his dad says to him. He nods his head and leans it back onto my shoulder.

"Is that for me?" Carter asks, nodding toward the pie.

I nod, holding it up to him. He takes the

plate and holds it up to his nose. "Blackberry? What's the special occasion?"

He takes big bites of the pie, and I watch him enjoy it. "No special occasion. I just thought you'd need sustenance."

I take the empty plate from him and look over at the other men. None of them seem to be paying any attention to us. "Yeah, I'm about to put CJ down for a nap and I thought you'd want to come to the house for a little while."

I can feel my face heat as I say it, but I'm not ashamed to admit I want my husband. Sometimes I can sit on the porch for hours and watch him ride his horse. I've never seen a grander sight.

He leans down on the horse and jumps off the side before climbing the fence and meeting me on my side. He puts his arm around me and hollers over his shoulder, "Take care of the horses. I'll be back."

I'm speechless, knowing that no matter what he's doing, he still puts my needs first. CJ coos at him, and he lifts him from my hip and carries him in his arms. "You know, you don't have to bring me pie. If you need me, all you have to do is say the word. I'm yours."

I quicken my step, and he does the same. "Fine. I need you."

As soon as he walks in the door, he points toward our bedroom. "Give me five minutes to get the little guy down. I'll be right there."

I kiss CJ on the forehead and walk into our bedroom. I undress quickly and lie down on the bed. I don't even worry about hiding under the covers or anything like I once did. Carter has proven over and over that he loves my body just the way it is.

Barely any time passes, and Carter is in the room, kicking off his shoes and undressing at the speed of light. I raise up on my elbows and look at his hard manhood. "I guess you need me too."

He lies down on top of me, kissing me breathless. "Always, I'll always need you."

He doesn't stop there. He spends the next hour showing me how much he loves me and exactly how much he needs me.

Want more Cowboys Love Curves?

Whiskey Run is home to the sexiest and most possessive cowboys you'll ever find. They work hard and play even harder. They might be gruff and bossy, but all it will take is the right curvy woman to bring them to their knees. Welcome to Whiskey Run... where the cowboys know how to ride.

Get the series here: Cowboys Love Curves

Rescuer Cowboy by Mia Brody

Obsessed Cowboy by Hope Ford

Virgin Cowboy by Kat Baxter

Tempted Cowboy by Frankie Love

Committed Cowboy by Kaci Rose

Want more of Whiskey Run?

Whiskey Run

Faithful - He's the hot, say-it-like-it-is cowboy, and he won't stop until he gets the woman he wants.

Captivated - She's a beautiful woman on the run... and I'm going to be the one to keep her.

Obsessed - She's loved him since high school and now he's back.

Seduced - He's a football player that falls in love with the small town girl.

Devoted - She's a plus size model and he's a small town mechanic.

Whiskey Run: Savage Ink

Virile - He won't let her go until he puts his mark on her.

Torrid - He'll do anything to give her what she wants.

Rigid - If you love reading about emotionally wounded men and the women that help them overcome their past, then you'll love Dawson and Emily's story.

Whiskey Run: Heroes

Ransom - He's on a mission he can't lose.

FREE BOOKS

Want **FREE BOOKS?**

Go to www.authorhopeford.com/freebies

JOIN ME!

JOIN MY NEWSLETTER & READERS
GROUP

www.AuthorHopeFord.com/Subscribe

JOIN MY READERS GROUP ON
FACEBOOK

www.FB.com/groups/hopeford

Find Hope Ford at www.authorhopeford.com

ABOUT THE AUTHOR

USA Today Bestselling Author Hope Ford writes short, steamy, sweet romances. She loves tattooed, alpha men, instant love stories, and ALWAYS happily ever afters. She has over 100 books and they are all available on Amazon.

To find me on Pinterest, Instagram, Facebook, Goodreads, and more:

www.AuthorHopeFord.com/follow-me

Made in the USA
Columbia, SC
19 July 2024

38889683R00093